Nearing's Grace (1979)

Lifetime (1981)

Last Resort (1982)

Last Resort

LAST RESORT

A Novel by

Scott Sommer

Random House   New York

*Grateful acknowledgment is made to the following
for permission to reprint previously published
material:*
   Cherio Corporation: Lyrics from "Young at
Heart" by Carolyn Leigh & Johnny Richards. ©
1954 by Cherio Corporation. International
copyright secured. All rights reserved. Used by
permission.   Simon & Schuster: The definitions
of *adult* and *ripe* were taken, in abridged form
and with permission, from *Webster's New World
Dictionary*, College Edition. Copyright © 1968
by The World Publishing Co.   Courtesy of
Simon & Schuster, Inc.

Library of Congress Cataloging in Publication
Data
Sommer, Scott
Last resort.
I. Title.
PS3569.06533L3   813'.54   81–48280
ISBN 0–394–52290–7   AACR2

Manufactured in the United States of America

9 8 7 6 5 4 3 2

First Edition

FOR GLORIA AND GARY

He was unhappier than ever, so lonely
that he even started talking to his dog . . .

Said of Lord Byron, toward his end.

The author is pleased to acknowledge receipt
of a National Endowment for the Arts grant and
a Creative Artists Public Service Award.

Breakups

I

I DROPPED OFF LEAH AT DAWN ON THE TENTH DAY OF SUMMER.
She wouldn't let me help her with the suitcases. I watched her
carry them down the walk to her parents' doorstep; she didn't
once turn around. After seven years I don't think either one
of us ever imagined it ending like that.

The Buick's transmission died in the salt mist a block from
the ocean. Dennis didn't care. After sixteen years of rising
gasoline prices, and half that many breakdowns, I didn't give
a damn myself. I gazed hopelessly through the windshield at
the Atlantic. The horizon was gray and then lavender and then
violet; but it was the empty blue space of the death seat that
triggered my heartache.

I left the car smoking at the curb and walked toward the
water. The wind lashed sand as high as my ankles and the waves
crashed with the persistence of my confusions. How at twenty-
five my life had come to absolutely nothing was a mystery for
which I needed a clue. You get older, I suppose, and things
have a way of slipping through your fingers.

Still, as I had little choice, I was intent upon carrying on. I
undressed, knifed the first dirty swell and surfaced with the

ocean safely at shoulder level. It seemed to mean something—
for example, that I might live to tell about the perfect terror
of postindustrial peacetime.

Naturally, Dennis had run off with the towel. He was always
running off. Ten years old, he was shaking six dollars' worth of
magenta cotton from side to side while sprinting south after
shorebirds. I didn't shout for him, or whistle. Dennis does not
obey. Without him, however, there would be nothing between
me and my emotional abyss.

I wrapped myself in the sweat shirt of my anonymous alma
mater and stood shivering with crossed arms. From above, the
eyes of countless gulls assailed me. Undoubtedly they wondered why I hadn't left them in peace—free to scavenge the
chemicalized litter of crab amputations—until ten A.M. or so,
as did the normal coastline citizenry.

I let them know, emphatically, that I am nothing if not
abnormal.

Then the heartache of my amputation from Leah Summit
set me wondering about the meaning of those ephemeral al-
liances with others that had never once succeeded in getting
me away from myself. That I should be stuck with myself now
seemed one more injustice for which no earthly redress existed.

I closed my eyes to the wind and listened to the shorebirds'
calling.

In summary, I had returned home, after four years of absence, with neither excuse nor exoneration, with only a failure
as legible as a morning headline. It was a humiliation I had
dreaded for the better part of a decade, and one I had finally
accomplished without even lifting a finger.

QUITTING THE BEACH, I CROSSED OCEAN AVENUE AND PASSED
the Last Resort with its broken neon sign flashing ANCY. Sections of white paint had peeled from the hotel's walls and lay

like litter over the uncut lawn; and the once green awnings had gone gray with water stains. The realtor's red FOR SALE sign seemed my father's public acknowledgment that he had run the landmark successfully into the ground.

Two doors inland of the Last Resort stands the family house, where I was raised and, more than likely, ruined. It is a three-story Victorian mansion full of windows, with charcoal-gray cedar shingles and brick-colored roof tiles. Four summers earlier Leah Summit and I had painted every shingle and window-frame, tacked every roof tile; and not returned again.

Four summers later, though I wanted it to be true, neither Leah nor I were still painting the house. I opened my eyes and noted Grandma on the porch beneath her red comforter, rocking in her white wicker favorite. At eighty-eight, waiting to be a ghost, she looked every day of it.

I waved. She slid the binoculars from the nuthatch on the sycamore and spotted me, in full self-effacement, standing before the red WRONG WAY sign.

"How come Leah ain't with Sonny?"

I thought, how come indeed, and counted seven steps, all rotten, to the porch landing. Grandma either had been eating an orange or simply smelled like one.

"Visiting family," I said, and kissed her.

She pointed to the west. "I'd've sworn our Leah's family lived two blocks that way. Or is Grandma thinking of Mommy in Brooklyn?"

To confess the truth to the venerably disoriented on my first day home in four years seemed more hurtful than moral. I told Grandma that Leah was visiting friends, *friends,* in Pittsburgh, and she implored me with eyes exhausted by time. "Then Leah ain't coming for breakfast?"

I nodded. Grandma drifted away, inconsolable. Sunlight surmounted the house and struck the lawn, where dew sparkled sadly as tears. Dennis, meanwhile, shot off the porch, barking, to pursue a roller skater. Grandma frowned and aimed the binoculars at the skater, who was irresistible in satin shorts. I'd known the woman nearly my entire lifetime. She blew Grandma a kiss and the recognition signaled directly in the matriarch's face. "Sonny?"

My eyes dropped contritely.

"I'm surprised at my Sonny. I really is."

I sat down on the steps to confess and peered through the crumbling wood. "We've been fighting."

Grandma was in earnest. "Don't never fight, Sonny. People die when we never know. Grandpa had a wonderful disposition but died faster than it takes to turn a pancake."

I was staring into the road, considering Leah's increasing distance, when Grandma said, "It ain't fair to break Grandma's heart. She baked all week."

I mounted my father's bicycle and gave chase. There was nothing to say, of course. We'd been through it all. I'd told Leah a month earlier that it was unendurable enough being single and without a clue, let alone without one and married. The wedding was off.

After two blocks I turned north to the family cottage, where everyone still assumed Leah and I would spend the summer together as hapless and wife.

THE TINY KITCHEN OF THE COTTAGE WAS SPICK-AND-SPAN FROM my mother's frantic janitorial efforts to make me and Leah comfortable therein and, implicitly at least, out of her hair. My mother is the sort of neurasthenic whose amiability diminishes in direct proportion to one's proximity and the length of time one remains proximate; her distemper surfaces in estimable degrees, and in the end her lid inevitably blows sky-high in a tirade of hysteria and paranoia. And now her son, at twenty-five, was suddenly unemployed, homeless and insufficiently commercial as a musician to attain himself official poverty level. Obviously he wasn't about to add "still single" to her conformist's list of disparagements.

I closed my eyes to a window full of sun and listened to the coffee percolating in the stainless-steel pot. Seven years was a long time together, and to say that the cottage wasn't filled with Leah's absence would be to lie. In my defense, I didn't realize I couldn't marry Leah until after we declared that we would. The world by itself is abundantly and inventively hurtful; why drag someone down with you if you sense you are drowning?

I poured the coffee and went to the yard. The fat man beneath the sombrero was pulling his model battleship behind him, atop a modified skateboard trailer. His eyes were lifeless and almond-shaped, which signified, to me, that he was eating Libriums like they were M & Ms.

"Looking for Aldo Bottoms."

"You know damn well he answers to Tramp."

He looked at me skeptically through one eye before offering me his hand: We touched for the first time in four years. Then I crossed my arms in a reflex of self-protection as he wondered out loud if he'd ever live long enough to see my hair the length of a normal son's. I feared he was resurrecting the tiresome and let him know it. He nodded shamefully and gazed into the trees.

"Meanwhile, Junior, on my end of the shaft, business is dead. I want that resort sold yesterday. Sign says closed for *repair* only because the sign people misspelled *despair*. Then there's your mother worse than ever, and your sister's life with the retarded still a complete mystery to me. On the upside there's the Pee Wee Regatta at season's end. After that, just about nothing."

He pushed a button on the Futura transmitter box and the engine blades of his miniature boat buzzed like a fly. "Marriage

has many pains," he volunteered, "but celibacy has no pleas-
ures. As usual, your father loses both ways."

In the road a woman with a bandanna round her head, a
bluejay feather fastened in back, roller-skated past. Her hair
was long and black and she winked a gorgeous gray eye at me.
Dennis was jogging alongside her. The day went silent and I
was abandoned to summer, to the enveloping smell of the
ocean. When I turned back to him, my father handed me a
sheet of paper. "You don't demonstrate a proprietary interest
to my satisfaction, I'll shut off the gas and electric. We understand one another?"

The sheet was entitled "Projects" and numbered 1 to 10.

"As ever," I said.

"I didn't think so." Turning away, he muttered, "Fare thee
well, lad," and foundered down the driveway, hauling his
model yawl behind him. It was clear from the gradational
discoloration of his shorts' seamline that my mother had let out
his Bermudas for a third straight summer.

I OWN A SURFBOARD, AN ASSEMBLY-LINE POP-OUT, A BAHNE BY
name and do not know how to surf upon it. The board under
my arm, I sauntered seaward. Then I remembered Grandma,
her diminishing claim on the world, and phoned from the
beach to cancel our breakfast engagement. Instead, my mother
answered sleepily from her bed of one psychosomatic illness
after the other.

"Mother?"

"Doctor?"

"It's Tramp."

"I don't know any Dr. Tramp."

"Tramp, your son."

"My son is Aldo Huxley Bottoms."

"He changed seven years ago into Tramp."

"I'm so terribly sorry to hear that."

"Would you be kind enough to inform Grandma that her grandson will not be home for breakfast?"

"Are you phoning from the road?"

"I'm phoning from the beach."

"Beach? Does that mean you're vacationing somewhere? Because we had you scheduled this summer for the cottage, which we could have rented for well over one thousand dollars. Since, however, you and Leah needed a handout, we thought a major sacrifice on our part wouldn't go unappreciated."

"Hometown beach."

"Hometown? Here? Then we can expect you for breakfast."

I went over it once more, slowly; in the process I heard the match of my mother's cigarette flare like a sigh.

"It's going to be an insufferable summer, dear," she said, "unless I get some cooperation. Your grandmother needs rest-home attention and I so wish you'd support me on this issue."

I stared down treeless Ocean Drive. Wind lashed sunlight against the row of old white mansions, and a piece of newspaper sailed into a parking meter. Somehow, once again I was standing in my old hometown, the very heartland of my malaise.

"Good-bye now, Mother."

"I'm so sorry you awakened me, dear, aren't you? You're really so much like your father, who's just a complete stranger to me, even after thirty-four years of marriage. Try not to do this sort of thing again."

"You may trust," I concluded, "that I will not."

AT NOON I EMERGED FROM THE WATER WITH MY BOARD. I HAD surmounted it but once, and then for less than three seconds. I was wearing a wet-suit top and my hair was appropriately long and blond, so I looked the part, assuming you didn't *watch* me. Leah's father, Wharton Summit, all bones, wearing an olive stretch bathing suit and a pair of yellow radiophones clamped over his ears, was fishing at shore for bass. On weekdays the man hauled nuclear waste for a utility company. According to the doctors, the work had finally gotten into his blood. But when we shook hands I detected a trace of victory in his smile.

"Leah told us this morning," he shouted above the waves. "Can't say I'm unhappy. Not after you never tried to mend fences with Mrs. S. after you cursed her down via phone on engagement night."

I smiled, patting his bony shoulder. "You're just an idiot who hauls fallout in leaky cans. I'm hopeful you'll be dead by Christmas, God forgive me."

He propped his rod in its stand and removed the radiophones. "Can't hear a word, boy."

I nodded my enmity. "I said I must look like an idiot falling off my board and God knows I'll probably die trying."

Mr. Summit savored that bit of self-disparagement. "You never could do much very well. Your music is ugly and you got an attitude about yourself being better than others that just about stinks out any nice home you step into." He shook my hand and returned the radiophones to his ears. "You're just another kid gone off the track with the majority," he shouted. "You're not family in my book and I'm sure it's vice versa with you."

Well, I merely waved good-bye. All I wanted was avocado and cucumber on whole wheat.

A woman lay in my path on a bright-red towel. She was tan and slim, with long black hair and gray eyes. You could search your entire lifetime for such hip bones and never find them.

"You'll get picked up for indecency," I told her.

"I am twenty-five years old and now unattached." She sounded awfully sad.

"Leah?"

"You're standing in my sun, Tramp." Her eyes were closed.

"Please, put on your top. This is a family beach."

She opened one eye and spoke very softly. "You've broken my heart and I'm so angry that I'm afraid I want to hurt you back."

"I'm sick about what's happened. You must believe that."

"I don't want to talk anymore."

I didn't once turn around. I got as far as the boardwalk before I noticed my father signaling with his arms from the mezzanine roof of the resort. I put my hands to my ears and the damn fool hoisted my sister's old cheerleader megaphone to his mouth.

"Come to the aid of your keeper, Junior, on the double!"

I raised my middle fingers, a twin gesture of dishonor, and set off for lunch with Grandma.

NAME SOMEONE WHO HAS GRADUATED FROM THEIR TRICYCLE not demented with grief. I looked at myself in the hallway mirror of the house and confessed that I certainly was not one. For her part, Grandma was sleeping at the kitchen table. Above her, sunlight poured through a skylight and illuminated six place settings with name tags: Grandma, Mommy, Daddy, Leah, Teresa, Sonny. If I was looking for clues, I'd come to the right address.

There was no chair for Teresa, just an emptiness where dust swirled silently in sunlight, awaiting a wheelchair. Yet the table itself was filled with croissants, strawberry jam and a bowl of sliced fruit, and upon the stove, in the darkness of a corner, sat a pot of coffee, doubtless several hours old.

When Grandma goes over, goes into the dark, I shall move

up one, come one person closer. Her croissants, the secret recipe, will go with her. I sat down, bit into one, and Grandma lifted her head. Objectively she was just an old woman with a cupboardful of pots and pans and a family for which she would receive no awards. Yet to me her existence hinted at the possibility of a creator.

"Good morning, Whito!" Whitney is my father's name. I let it pass.

Crumbs fell from my mouth. "I'm starving, Grandma."

She shook her head and pressed her lips together mournfully. "Sometimes, Sonny, when I think of that crash, I just got to go to my room like I'm sleepy and cry in my pillow."

I reached for a second croissant and Grandma went to the stove as naturally as I go to the piano. By the time she returned with the heated coffee, I had finished two wedges of honeydew melon. That crash. Scotty dead and my sister crippled. Sometimes I cry into my pillow too.

"I ain't telling you or Leah what I got you two for a wedding present, but it's the nicest thing I ever got anybody in my life."

I watched her pouring the coffee. "Grandma?"

"Mommy wants the ceremony in the living room so we got the sun away from the wedding cake. She's got a guest list of fifty and Mrs. Summit invited more than that. I'm making the same cheesecake Grandma Cookie made for my wedding." She completed her pouring and looked at me. "Ain't it something how fast a life is, Sonny?"

"Grandma, there's something—"

"It'll be a beautiful ceremony after Mommy gets done planning. She used to be a decorator before she couldn't help from screaming at her customers." Grandma sat beside me, holding the coffee pot, and gazed into her lap. "Teresie would have been married by now if Scotty hadn't lost the wheel. He was such a handsome boy, so nice and polite. So clean!"

"There's something I should tell you, Grandma."

"Daddy don't want to pay for no band, but Mommy already got one." Grandma referred to her little wristwatch. "Where the hell's Leah already?"

"I've been trying to tell you about Leah and me, Grandma."

Well, she spotted it in my eyes and bowed her head again. "I get so sleepy this time of day," she whispered, and I watched her rush to the refrigerator, open the door absently and then move to the stairway.

"Grandma?"

"I got to rest my legs."

When I spread the comforter over her on the bed, she removed her glasses and stared dumbly at me. "Leah's the only good thing you ever done for yourself, Sonny."

I kissed her cheek and stepped into the hallway. My mother emerged from her darkened room in her nightgown and drifted toward the bathroom with her hands sliding along the hallway walls. I assumed a migraine had forced her eyes closed. The advantage, obviously, was that I remained undetected in my flight from the house.

SHIRTLESS, AND BUSILY SMOKING A CIGAR, MY SO-CALLED keeper was standing on the roof staring at two broken skylights. He wore his yellow Bermudas and sombrero. The sun, severe as my mother's temper, threatened to burn his beer gut to a crisp.

"So long as I've known you, Junior, you've had two speeds. Slow and stop."

"What is it this time, Father?"

He flicked cigar ashes into the sea breeze.

"This time you've got skylights leaking on the beds in 3A and 3B. I expect the project completed by sundown."

My father placed his hand on my shoulder. "Confidentially speaking, Junior, I've become a disheartened son of a bitch because I'm fed up with everyone I know, not necessarily withstanding you. There's not a damn thing personal about it. People can't help themselves, I know this. I'll even admit that I'm not a happy man from my own doing, but does that mean everyone I know has to make it worse? Which brings us to something I want to discuss with you."

Above the Atlantic a little red plane was hauling a sign that read DISCO YOUR BRAINS OUT AT THE BEACHFRONT KAFE. It seemed a good idea, though obviously there was now the problem of a partner. True, heartache could always accompany me, but she tended to step on your face.

"You listening to me, Junior, or dreaming about what might have been had you only listened a whole lot sooner?"

"Listening."

"Well, this is strictly between you and me. You're the first I've told. So I hope you rejoice over the glad tidings that I am leaving your mother."

I averted my eyes to my feet, which were sinking into the roof's melting tar surface. "I have nothing to say."

"Your father's got thirty good ones left—if you follow me."

"I have done my very best not to, Father."

He removed his hand from my shoulder. "I never asked for admiration, Junior, just the honor God says Dad's got coming to him."

Our eyes met. I said, "Was there any one thing that made up your mind?"

My father considered the matter solemnly. "I'll put it this way, Junior: Have you any idea what foreplay is like with your mother?"

"Naturally, Father, I do not."

"Well, it's the goddamnedest twenty minutes of begging and pleading imaginable."

I looked to my feet again.

"About those skylights . . ."

I located two new panes in the downstairs lobby and set to work ambitiously, wondering about the transparency of our own pains, old and new, and the unmerciful inevitability of their replacement, one after the other.

THE RETIREE IN THE OCEAN GROVE RUNNERS CLUB BOOTH AN-nounced I had one last chance to register for the Ocean County Marathon. I stopped running long enough to fill out the form and part with my last twenty. When we hit the beach, Dennis went the other way. I realized why only after I spotted my mother sitting in a beach chair with her back to the sun, facing the waves. After four years of absence I couldn't run past her.

My mother's circulation is not good. The temperature registered ninety-two in the shade, yet her hand was as cold as ice when we shook hello.

"Even the children are worse," she said, and we watched three little acquisitors shovel starfish into their respective buckets. Thereafter I searched for my mother's eyes behind the veil of her sunglasses.

"How have you been, Mom?"

"How have I been, dear? Oh, I suppose I've never felt so unspeakably alone in all my life."

My mother's brown hair was shorter and thinner than I remembered, and was now full of gray.

"You see, dear, I have lived for over thirty years with a stranger who never loved me and who convinced me that somehow this was my fault. The redeeming thing, however, about a life of horrible loneliness is that it teaches you to trust yourself above all others. Perhaps this is indiscreet of me, but your father is impotent and blames me."

"Well," I said, "I'm in training for the Ocean County Marathon. I'll be off."

"Years ago, perhaps," my mother resumed, "I might have accepted this verdict as indisputable. Now, however, I realize that the man didn't really marry me so much as simply employ me without pay to satisfy his sexual and domestic appetites and needs." She paused to clear her throat.

I said, "I don't know why everyone is unhappy. I wish they weren't. Now I've got to run."

"I feel so estranged from that insufferable father of yours, dear, that I'm afraid I shall simply kill myself if I don't throw him out of the house. He'll just have to find other accommodations. Are you listening to me?"

I turned my attention from the coastline. My mother was rummaging through her beach bag for a cigarette. It took her seven matches to get the filter lit. I helped her light the second one correctly.

"Finally," she said, exhaling, "there are my own two hellish creations—my ungrateful and self-centered children, who either indict me or mollify me but never express any love for me. The truth is, my life has been a terrible series of undeserved interpersonal disasters."

The tide had drifted out and the gulls were scavenging in the calm of late afternoon.

"It's been a very long day, Mom. My first one home in four years."

"Every day is long, dear. They get longer and longer each day we live." She looked up from her hands. "Now I shall tell you something you must never communicate to anyone else. Can you keep a secret, dear?"

"It's going to storm, Mother. See?" I pointed to the horizon.

"Your father once gave me crabs. This was *after* we were married."

I sighed and closed my eyes. When I opened them my

mother blew smoke from her nose and waved her hand at the world.

"Well, it doesn't matter to me anymore, dear. I'm going to have my hair dyed and my entire face lifted in California, including a nose job and perhaps a tummy tightening. But you must promise not to tell a soul, and perhaps now that I've mentioned this to you, you should promptly forget it. Actually I'm exhausted from arguing with you for twenty-odd years and suggest we knock it off immediately."

I studied my mother, sitting at the very edge of the continent in short pants and a sweater, and then I ran like hell to the north.

. . . After ten miles I tend to forget that we move one step at a time through a sphere of being where the gun barrel of mortality is aimed directly at our hearts.

I WAS WALKING INLAND WHEN SOMEONE TAPPED ME ON THE shoulder. The sweat was beginning to chill on me, and as I turned, a spray flew from my face. The man's brown hair had gone gray at the sides; and his aggrieved eyes were the same startling color of faded blue as his workshirt. He handed me a business card:

RENAISSANCE

ANTIQUE AND REFINISHED FURNITURE

ELIOT HOWARD

MAIN STREET

OCEAN GROVE

"I'm so poor I can't buy my dog a flea collar," I said, and returned the card to him.

"I have some nice inexpensive things you might like," he said bashfully. "Please, keep the card." Then he offered me his hand. "I opened the store only this week. You're the first person I've approached. My name's Eliot Howard."

"My name's Dennis," I replied. "I've just run ten miles. No offense, but if I don't shower, I'll grow consumptive and die before my prime, like Jack Keats." I began walking toward the cottage.

"I used to run in high school," Eliot said, following. "Do you run very often?"

I told him every afternoon, like clockwork; since the truth of my ways is jejune, I tend to exaggerate. For his part, he gazed nervously at the sidewalk before inquiring if he might join me from time to time. A normal American, I am homophobic. I told him grudgingly that he could find me performing stretching exercises at the Fourth Avenue snack stand at four o'clock.

"Thanks very much, Dennis." He took my hand again. "I'm new in town, living in a motel."

I was staring down the block in the very direction he was pointing. "I'm beginning to chill, Eliot," and trotting away, I thought: The man is as vulnerable as a jugular vein at a cocktail party of straight razors.

That night, for the first time, I slept with my estrangement from Leah Summit.

II

A WEEK PASSED, DURING WHICH LEAH EVADED ME AND CHIL-
dren discharged explosives in celebration of the violence that
all independence requires of the dependent.

I woke to the first Monday of July in a state of horror.
Dennis was standing at the open window amid the curtain's
flurry, staring into the miracle of summer. Thereafter only my
terrible mind . . . the ceiling.

Naturally, reviewing the best times only makes the worst
times worse. Still, without that abundant sense of loss endemic
to memory, we wouldn't be distinguishable from Dennis, or a
bus rusting in a field.

I grew up with Leah Summit and went with her to college,
where we lived together in an old white house. Leah won the
university's venerable journalism award our senior year and I
dropped out, with seven incompletes, to form my band. At the
time I was twenty-two and would have bet the ranch that by
twenty-five I'd be the nation's singing savior. The world, however, was not created to respect every punk's dream of salva-
tion.

For three years the Tramp Bottoms Band established my

anonymity, nothing more. In the interim Leah acquired a master's degree and sold four articles on animal exploitation to national magazines. I composed and engineered as many demo tapes and sent each of them to dozens of record-company A & R minions. The best one, *Rock Bottom*, solicited variations on the same lame theme:

> Bottoms is good; alas, his singing lacks range, assurance and color, and his melodies tend to blur together. The lyrics, however, knocked me out! Try again.

> Bottoms *is* someone to watch—maybe. Right now, however, his lyrics range from ardent declarations of love to inaccessibly weird expressions of puerile hostility.

Around that time I succumbed to six years of Mrs. Summit's incessant bitching about our singularly tentative life style, and Leah and I announced our engagement. It seemed a harmless formality to mollify Leah's inherited enslavement to respectability, something I loathe—as I have never been able to acquire it on my own terms. In the end, precisely because I tried to please everyone, I infuriated them all, especially Leah. She didn't believe me when I confessed that I loved her too much to abide her marrying me.

Well, my mind . . . the ceiling. Dennis still standing at the window, his head craned to me, question marks in his brown eyes. Certainly there were no answers in mine.

I sat up with the pronouncement, "Great day to achieve!" Dennis commenced chasing his tail and I suspected the bastard of mockery. I got two steps from bed before stepping in it.

My foot was in the sink when the doorbell rang. I answered in the terry-cloth robe Leah had bought me for my twenty-fifth birthday.

"What is that odor?"

"Dennis's *business.*"

I gazed at my sister, my twin, seven seconds younger than I. She certainly did seem frailer after a year in the wheelchair.

"Feeling better today, Mr. Bottoms?"

"Slight headache, Mrs. Bottoms."

When we were six Leah married us in a secret ceremony amid a rainstorm. My sister's sorrel hair still fell in curls to her frail shoulders, and she was still wearing a plain white dress.

"Want to talk about last night?" she said.

"Last night?"

"You showed up at the house in quite a state."

"Last night," I muttered, and tried to find the answer in the tree branches above my sister.

"Don't you remember sitting on the porch dead drunk screaming at Mommy and Grandma and me?"

My brain cannot function first thing without caffeine. I wheeled Teresa to the eastern side of the house, to the sun, and stepped into the kitchen. The coffee was a day old but, twice burned, tasted at least a week. The power of it set my brain percolating after two sips.

"Sometimes," I said, "it's impossible to believe that the past won't ever come back," and sitting beside my crippled sister, I lifted my face to the sun.

"Mr. Bottoms?"

I opened one eye. My sister is as delicate and beautiful as an angel. I am sentimental about her because she is my twin who lost the boy she loved and the use of her legs—all on the same day—and has never once, in a year's time, complained about it.

"Wasn't Daddy there?" I asked.

"I haven't seen Daddy in four days. None of us has."

"Well," I said, "I don't feel hung over. None of the usual attenuations." At which point a hangover lifted its hammer and began pounding a pipe in my brain.

"You called everyone names," my sister said. "You told

Mommy she was a passive-aggressive shrew and that Grandma was manipulative. Then you threatened to kill yourself if the family didn't leave you alone."

I returned my face to the sun.

"Grandma started crying."

I said slowly, "I have been under strain, Mrs. Bottoms. Personal and professional in nature."

"You also told us you and Leah weren't getting married."

"Nolo contendere."

"You realize you've broken everyone's heart?"

"Including my own leaky one."

"We all love Leah. You complement one another."

"Naturally. I'm bad, she's good."

I missed with the coffee; down my chin and onto my chest. I mopped up with the robe.

"Are you an alcoholic now, Aldo?"

"Still working on it."

My sister bowed her head, as she does when she's mad. "What are your plans for the summer?"

"*Plans?* You in cahoots with Mrs. Summit?"

"I am simply your infinitely patient sister, who has come here at the expense of being terribly late for work."

I turned again to the sun. "My plans are to succeed in my chosen field."

"Music?"

"Become the nation's singing savior by Christmas."

"So you've come back to be near Manhattan?"

"Also, I've no money to speak of, not to mention that my band dissolved last month at the same time the landlord refused to renew the lease."

"Did Leah come back to be near you?"

"Leah came back," I said quietly, "to find a publisher for her book in progress on the nonhuman holocaust and to be with her father, who's very sick. No more questions now, please."

"May I suggest something?"

"I am not—*never*—going into the hotel business!"

"Go to the house for breakfast and apologize to Grandma."

Well, despite the fact that people die when you never know, I refused. Teresa said, "You've changed," and activated the wheelchair's motor. I said, "You're darn right," and watched her roll away.

I DUSTED OFF ARMATRADING WITH A SOCK AND BLASTED "LOVE and Affection." Dennis leaped up and we danced around. Sometimes it helps. Because I do not like, I positively dread, calling record companies. You want them to call you, to ring your doorbell·with a contract in hand, but they never do. I had specific people in mind, people who had heard my demo tapes before, but I couldn't circumvent their secretaries. I never can. They said, respectively: Call back; She's moved to the Coast; He's passed away.

So I lay vanquished with Dennis. The world was outside the window: bird noises, a lawnmower, wind in the dry leaves. Once I had a band and taught children how to play guitar and piano. I earned my keep. Then the band failed to evolve, and broke up, as did its leader.

I turned to Dennis. "Tell me I'm going to make it."

He was asleep, however, dreaming, undoubtedly, of Milk Bones. I closed my eyes and dreamed of a black vinyl disc— my lyrics, my picture, on a handsome jacket.

I sat up. The *Village Voice* was filled with announcements of sold-out concerts and advertisements of smash LPs. I turned to the little blocks of circled showcase bulletins, played eenie, meenie, minie, moe before my index finger landed on the End. When I phoned I was told that Monday was indeed audition night, though only the first ten people on the list would be granted a *hearing*. "Ask for Owen Chance," the voice said, and hung up.

Dennis opened one eye at the box spring's creaking but didn't come along. So I walked to the Last Resort alone, save my entourage of fears, to entreat my father for the Avanti. There wasn't a single name in the hotel register. The lobby and hallways were cluttered with beds, old furniture and worn rugs. I searched all three floors before I discovered him on the roof, nine sheets to the wind beneath his sombrero. Needless to say, those sad eyes, that abject smile. He held a radio transmitter for his model airplane and pointed to the sky. I observed the glittering toy shooting toward the sun.

"Since you're out and about without my permission, I assume we've finished our seven steps."

"Have yet to lift a finger."

He put the beer to his lips and drank without moving his eyes from the plane. "Let me put it this way: If you're figuring to lift a finger at my dinner table tonight, you'll need a written note from me. This will demand ingratiation. You will improve your position by phoning the electric-company people at once. Give them the address of the cottage and instruct them to terminate power until you've repaired the steps in question. Then return to my side for a serious conference in which I will possess another distinct competitive advantage."

"I need the car tonight," I said patiently. "Strictly business."

"Business? How's this for business: no wedding in my home for you and your only redeeming feature until my steps are completed."

I pointed into the afternoon's vacuum. "You're fast approaching Mrs. Zwillman's TV antenna."

My father commanded the Concorde miniature toward a cumulonimbus before he terminated the power. The plane died in mid-ascent and nose-dived in silence toward the beach.

The three-foot wingspan cast an extended shadow, and a gaggle of swimsuits began to scatter with the lifeguard's first whistle. My father then restored power, directing the plane to sea. Regrettably, he lost himself in a dive-bombing raid on a tourist fishing boat, and the plane was snared by a fishing line, went momentarily berserk, crashed through the mainsail of a catamaran and plunged disastrously into the Atlantic.

I was standing beside the pilot—thinking, why me?—when he yanked me behind a chimney, through an open sliding door and into his new retreat. I looked heavenward to admire the skylights, which I had successfully installed the previous week.

"That plane was a south Jersey champion. I'm devastated by the loss. May I offer my only son a beer?"

"Look it, I'm going to Manhattan and need your car!"

"Finish those seven steps by sundown!"

"We've been all through this. Where are the keys?"

He tossed them to me in a parabola of jingling. The key-ring slogan: I DON'T WANT TO DRINK, I HAVE TO DRINK.

"Have you told your wife you're leaving her?"

"She'll catch on."

Exasperation makes me look toward God's purported hideaway. Two pigeons were immersed in a foreplay cha-cha on the skylight.

"In case you're interested," I said, "I'm going to Manhattan tonight in search of my musical dream."

"Junior," he said imperviously, "after sliding down the razor blade of life for fifty-plus years, I simply don't have the strength to fight another war with that woman."

"So long."

"Listen," he said, grabbing me. "When a man can't perform with his wife, he's got a problem. Not a sex problem per se, but a sex problem per his wife. You know damn well that I'm not the sort of man to follow his lower instincts from one woman to the next, but there's nothing like a dysfunctional apparatus to bring out the worst in a man."

"In conclusion," I said, turning away, "I have to go now."

"I'm confident the problem is *specific,*" he said, following me, "because it goes up each time one catches my eye. Even so, Daddy's been loyal to Junior's mom for thirty-odd years. Confidentially, it's the regret of his lifetime."

I stepped onto the roof and stared down the steps. I was halfway down when I noticed a shadow eclipse my own. I turned. My father stood at the summit.

"Just remember who gave it to you straight!"

Well, it was sad—my father slipping into incoherence without any semblance of Lear's pathos.

"I can't tell you," I said, "how much I wish you hadn't."

The Avanti was below me, backed into the fencing surrounding the hotel pool. The key fit the ignition but there were problems: one dead battery, two flat tires.

"Drive carefully!" My father waved into the storm of my disgust.

THE RAILROAD CLERK SAID THE FOUR-THIRTY ARRIVED IN NEW York City at six o'clock. I restrung my Gibson, stuffed two oolong tea bags into my jeans and slipped on my epicene blouse of crimson silk. Halfway to the station I remembered forgetting to kiss Dennis good-bye. I went back, found him drinking from the toilet and acknowledged the general error of my sentiments.

According to the conductor, an Amtrak express ahead of our local Conrail had killed someone clowning on the tracks in Elizabeth. The delay lasted twice as long as my patience. The little fatty across the aisle chanted, "Show us the bod-ee! Show us the bod-ee!" The mother was an immigrant blimp consuming one seat per varicose leg. The two of them had been employed in a disgusting goat-cheese-and-onion festival, and a blood-on-the-tracks death seemed precisely the cake and ice cream their little party had been lacking.

I reached the end of my rope just about the time the train pulled into Penn Station. What comes over me is a sense of morbid isolation and futility. Outside the cab window Manhattan seemed a skyscraper mausoleum crawling with ghouls. Bleecker Street, however, was more down-to-earth, with all the quaintness of a stag-film gang bang; and the End was just another façade in the Village's carnival grotesquery. The ride cost five dollars.

Inside the End, Owen Chance was eating cheesecake by candlelight. The coiffed hair seemed a stylized extension of the tweezed eyebrows, and his batik jump suit was three shades of opalescent green.

"I'm awarding you number seven," he said, "because I adore your top. My name's Owen and I'm very picky. Funnily enough, 'Tramp Bottoms' has a kind of punky resonance that makes me want to know a whole lot more about him."

Well, I got away from there with a homophobic purposefulness. I sat at the bar with the other aspirants and ordered a shot of vodka, a cup of hot water and a glass of ice. By the time I had the oolong concoction mixed, a breathless woman in red vinyl pants had completed her shrill rock 'n' roll assault. The best part of her act had been the ringing telephone, the bartender clinking glasses and the police car's Gestapo sonata. I watched the daylight fade into gloom.

I came on with the streetlights. Owen said, "Tramp now," and I headed for the piano. The blue spotlight illuminated the keyboard and my presence. Owen said, "Your life is on the line. Go for it." I thought of my first quarter century on earth and lit into "Crazy for Free."

I can't forget toxic waste
The nuclear arms race
The void surrounding the brain
But nothing ventured
Nothing gained
Death takes us from home in a box

Yeah, you live for me
And I'll go crazy for you
Your dream might become
My nightmare too
I'm no more real than you think

I'll be a skeleton one day
A box of bones with nothing to say
But first I've gotta sing my life down
I want them to immortalize my cassette
Not shovel mud all over my casket

I'm prepared to live with you
If you'll live with me
It won't be long
Before we're gone
Might as well die trying

Well, they sit there, they stare at you. Through the window
traffic passes in the street. I switched to the guitar for "Brain-
Damaged Heart."

Sometimes I think the sun and rain
Exist just to traumatize our brain
So we live
From year to year
Age from far to near
Death sticks it in our ear

No wonder we
Get nasty
Go mad
Die on our backs

Hey, no head mechanic can explain
Only sends a monthly bill
Prescribes a barbiturate pill
But I'm afraid what ills me
Won't cease till it kills me
I need more than a 'lude job

No, this isn't school
So don't test my brain
Question whether it's insane
I dropped out due to pain

World's too much day after day
Makes you feel too far away
Life's a clock
Our heart's a target

Oh yes, we get
Nasty
We go mad
We die too late

I finished to traffic horns and a tray crashing in the kitchen. When I stepped clear of the blue light, Owen said, "A macabre sense of rockability!" and winked.

I thought, all I have ever wanted throughout my entire life is a woman like Leah and a glass room full of sunlight. Nonetheless, I lamented this while drinking a final vodka in a dungeon of exhausted air and nutritional suicide.

After the girl outfitted in dungaree finished her ode to the clitoral orgasm, Owen called us into the kitchen one at a time. Naturally, when the first six emerged you could tell by the expressions what had been decided between the sink and the salad table. When I went in, seventh, Owen said, "Look here, to be perfectly frank, I think you are fabulously promising. How's next Monday at ten-thirty?"

I asked if I could have a half hour to myself.

He said, "I happen to know people in this city who would happily pay you big bone for half an hour."

I have lived the better part of my life with Leah, with Dennis. I am not hip.

"Record people?" I asked.

"Certainly record people. But they'd only love you for your machine. Do you understand?"

I suspected that I did. The last thing I said was, "Ten-thirty Monday," and fled.

I hugged my guitar the entire ride through the ravished Jersey flatlands. Through the train window Perth Amboy was a horrifying civic autopsy, but I was on my way again—a New York City showcaser with an obsessive resiliency. If I was going to fail, losing Leah and my life, then I would make them drag me, kicking and scratching, off the floor of my demise.

III

I LEFT ONE PHONE MESSAGE AFTER ANOTHER. THE SUMMITS SAID Leah was meeting with an editor in Manhattan. I expected a call after two days but didn't get one. Finally I sent a telegram.

COULD YOU COME HOTEL MONTANA MADRID. AM RATHER IN TROUBLE.
BRETT.

Well, nothing for another day, and at that point I wasn't going to run after her, certainly would not show up at the Beachfront Kafe, where, Mrs. Summit informed me, she was working. At night I wrote "Bitch on Wheels"; by daylight I approached the repair of seven goddamn steps with all the eagerness of a claustrophobic approaching a tunnel entrance.

On Friday I spotted the source of my sorrow. I was sitting at the curb, watching the sun sink, when she wheeled past in a streak of silver. As she pirouetted on white roller skates with exotic red wheels, I knew what it was like to be a dog without a bone.

"It's just heartbreaking for me to see a man your age sitting like this on a street corner."

She was wearing too much eye makeup, and her Kafe outfit left too little to the public's imagination. I lowered my eyes, and my hands fumbled through the gutter litter of bottle caps and amber shards of glass. "I've dropped the key to my life's little riddles somewhere around here."

"Poor Brett."

"Leah, I've made a terrible mistake."

"Of course you have, Weepy. You could have been a man with a beautiful and intelligent wife with an advance of fifteen thousand dollars on a forthcoming book about animal exploitation."

"What!"

"Instead you have chosen to dump her and string yourself out in a seaside street gutter. I signed the contract yesterday. What's with our boy?"

"Our boy's an archetypal case of retarded development looking for a shortcut into adulthood."

"If you're going to write lyrics at me, I'm leaving."

The sun sailed away and I was left in the dark. I cried "Stop!" and Leah twirled gracefully on all eight wheels. The street lamps snapped to full illumination and my shadow nearly reached her. I could hear the ocean crashing regimentally across the road.

"Why are you working at the Kafe?"

"To keep my mind off the truth that something horrible has happened between me and someone I used to know."

"Leah?"

"Sweetheart, I miss us as much as you do."

"I'm afraid of ruining your life."

"Darling, I'm afraid what you really want is to screw sleazo chippies."

"That's your story of what went wrong, not mine."

"Personally, I just wish you'd go ahead and get it off your
. . . mind. In the meantime I'm going to throw my advance
into a little wooden house where I can write my book in peace."

I called, but she didn't stop. The phosphorescent red snake
stitched to her back disappeared down the avenue. She was a
moving violation on her way to service disco geeks intent upon
a night-long frenzy of copulatory foreplay, whereas I was a
piece of roadside litter fearful of being swept up and discarded.

Sleazo chippies had nothing to do with it.

I WANDERED TO THE OCEAN AND LOOKED UP. THE UNIVERSE WAS
filled with innumerable little lights, and the coppery moon was
rising above the waves. The mystery of it all went right over
my head. I knew, however, where my earthly reward was situated, and looked south, down the miles of beach, to the Kafe.
The lights of Asbury Park seemed more like Kafka's version of
Oz than Dorothy's, and I remembered once again that Leah
couldn't save me from myself.

Still, I ran all the way and paid the price of admission with
a combination of coins.

I slid into the darkness enveloping the bar and scanned the
strobe-lit whirling for Leah. Fifteen thousand in advance
money and working tables to allay her sorrow! Well, the band
certainly wouldn't. Shrapnel and the Dementoids, no matter
how much volume they afflicted upon the New Wave fe-
tishists, were strictly shit on toast. Between songs the blonde
beside me asked if I would be her valentine and autograph her
"girlie place."

I let her know she was certainly pretty as they come, but that
I was a mental case in the throws of a malaise, if she followed.

She said into my ear, "I may be beautiful, but I get con-
stipated like everyone else."

I knew then, by the integument of ice on her eyes, that I

would contract frostbite of the instrument if we ever put it to each other.

"Hold my hand and I'll whisper you a secret," she said, and when I obeyed she whispered, "My name's Mrs. Anne Monroe, and Mr. Monroe is working late tonight. What's yours?"

"Murray Chase."

"Well now, Murray, I got a tight little number-one cookie and all you got to do to nibble on it is show up." She dropped her hand to my seat, and I said, removing it, "Sorry, Anne."

This evoked a change of tone. "Look it, Murray, my husband is the bartender here at the Kafe, and if you don't settle down real fast, he'll just kick your cock to Sioux City, Oklahoma, or thereabouts."

I glanced across the bar and spotted Mr. Monroe observing us with folded arms. Mrs. Monroe said, "I just know a boy handsome as you'll be much more careful from here on out."

Mr. Monroe put his rag to the bar's varnished gleaming. "What'll it be, Woodstock?"

This, I thought, is the twilight zone of a crumbling empire. I want to go home but cannot, as I no longer have a home. Yet somewhere on this planet, only in a different time zone, Leah Summit and I are cooking eggplant parmigiana in a kitchen with Dennis at our feet. There are curtains on the window and behind the curtains a yard with a garden full of lettuce. I must return to this place and chain myself to it.

Leah skated past in the darkness with a tray full of empty bottles. I had to say excuse me five times, fighting the crowd, before I reached her. When I grabbed hold of her from behind, she gasped and drew away.

"Leah, it's Tramp."

She whirled and glared. "Mister, I'm just a single woman working her way through a crass world of fools. You let go of my arm."

I said "Sorry" and, lowering my eyes, let her loose.

"It's going to get worse for you and you're all to blame. Go home."

"Haven't one."

"I work here to unwind and you're ruining it. Go to the boardwalk and win me something. A Raggedy Ann doll we can give to Teresa."

I lost five dollars' worth of quarters trying, then rode the Wild Mouse with delinquents before walking home, through a heavy ocean mist, on what was once called a promenade.

Dennis was rolled up on the pillow. His weeny, infected again, was leaking. But a dog, like a bed of flowers, like Leah's eyes, is a gift the world bestows upon us for free. I cut the bedroom light and he settled his head on my chest. I had a dog and a universe of supreme indifference to keep me company.

SOMETIME AROUND THREE A NOISE AT THE SCREEN WOKE ME. I sat up and whispered "Leah?" But when I opened the screen, the moth fluttered silently upwards, toward the bluish luminescence of the moon.

I lay awake listening to a train's warning horn. When it faded away to the north, toward New York City, I put on my robe and ran all the way to her house. Her light was on; her back was to me and she didn't once stop typing. She was wearing her lavender robe, and her hair was hanging down in a long black ponytail.

"Leah?"

"She's working."

"It's three in the morning."

"Later."

"Leah, please."

When she turned, she said tenderly, "Hello, you."

"Dennis ran away and I thought I might find him here."

"Sorry."

"Or a strange man."

"Only strange man in my life is you."

"May I come in?"

"Why, Tramp?"

"Because we each die faster than it takes to turn a pancake."

She unlatched the screen. "Don't disturb me. I've a dead-line."

I climbed in and went to the bed. I put the pillow over my head. When she picked it up, my eyes were wide open.

"Strange Tramp."

I put my head against her hip, and after a while she went back to her desk. I watched her work in the cone of lamplight and then I fell asleep. When I woke in the morning, she wasn't there. A note was resting in her typewriter: "Tramp darling, you'll never find anyone better."

A knock issued at the door and Mrs. Summit said, "Honey, your real estate man's on the phone." I had one foot out the window when she opened the door. I said vaguely, "Leah said I could," and ran off.

WHEN THE PHONE RANG AT THE COTTAGE, I SAID "LEAH!" AND my father shouted, "What about those goddamn steps!" I said "One second," and hung up. By the time it rang again, I had the coffee going. Just the smell helped. I dragged the phone onto the back stoop and put my face to the sun. I explained to my father that without his car I couldn't acquire the necessary lumber.

"Car's all set," he said, and hung up.

After my breakfast of coffee and iron filings, I found my father floating in the hotel pool in his white underpants and black snorkel and mask, scrubbing black algae from the pool walls. When he saw me he said, "Worthless!" The words piped up the snorkel extension, muting his bad temper, and fogged the mask. I located the car keys in his Bermuda pocket and he resumed his scrubbing.

Driving past the Summits' house, I had to brake to avoid Mr. Summit and his neighbor, Dominick Proscuto. The two were warring with gas-powered blowers in the middle of the street. Mr. Summit smiled broadly beneath his faded Marine Corps cap when he stepped to the side of the Avanti. He stood there, all skin and bone in his stretch bathing suit and Marine boots.

"This Sicilian SOB," he shouted above the machine's fury, "is a rich pig who thinks he can blow his waste in my face! I've got a machine here with ten horses in comparison to his three. He's lost and ashamed of himself, but won't give."

"I've got work to do," I said. "Get out of the road."

"I can't hear a word you're saying," he shouted. "Leah's got fifteen grand for herself now, and her mom and me just pray to Christ you'll stay the hell away now that she's proved why your type isn't hers."

I nodded at the machine. "I've hated you and your wife's guts for the better part of my life. She's always been a plastic bag over my head, and now, thank God, you're a dying man."

Mr. Summit leaned into the car. "Can't hear a frickin' word."

"If you'd take your wife along with you, maybe Leah and I might have more than a snowball's chance."

He shouted, "We can't take a vacation because I'm out on sick leave. I hate idleness bad as the next patriot and thought I'd show this rich SOB at whose property he can and cannot blow waste products."

I beeped twice and gunned the Avanti. The two horticultural technocrats retreated from the public roadway, and I sped off toward no place in particular.

I HAD THE SKELETON OF THE NEW STAIRWAY COMPLETED WHEN my mother, Vera Bottoms, walked onto the patio at two, fresh from her hiatus of twenty-two straight hours in bed. She examined the stairway to her domestic catastrophe with skepticism. Frankly, I could not blame her; it had never led one of us to any good.

She was drinking coffee and smoking a cigarette in a white plastic holder. Mercifully, her eyes were hidden behind green sunglasses. Less mercifully, her mouth was luminous with purple lipstick. I found her presence funereally disquieting, but then I tend to lack magnanimity. When she addressed me, her voice contained all the tremulous dread of a breakdown candidate without a sanitarium reservation.

"The next time you have the misfortune of seeing your father," she said, "you tell him he cannot use the laundry facilities in my house, nor the telephone for that matter. Neither can he read any part of the newspaper or magazines which are delivered here. And I'm disposing of his vulgar men's magazines with all those accommodating whores with whom he has always contrasted me in his sordid mind and with whom, I'm quite sure, he would love to replace me. Also, I will not accept any of his first-class mail into this house, so I recommend he complete a post office change-of-address form. Furthermore, you tell him that I've spoken to the lawyer about a divorce and will have the papers shortly. Are you listening, dear?"

I nodded, holding two nails between my teeth. The nails, I suppose, explained the metallic taste of dread.

My mother closed her eyes and inhaled smoke. A moment later it issued from her nose, like sports car exhaust, in two long plumes of gray. She stared at me and then eyed the empty roadway.

"Sometimes, Aldo, I confess I stare and stare at my bottles

of barbiturates and think, no, you mustn't do it, you must live for your ungrateful and self-centered children."

I reflected on her words and removed the poisonous nails. "How about some fresh orange juice and a couple of your Valiums?"

"You know, dear, to Camus suicide is the only pertinent philosophical issue."

"Perhaps," I said benignly, "you should contact your psychiatrist."

Mother, however, lost control. "I'm sick of so much criticism! Stop finding fault! Stop it, stop it, stop it!"

At once pigeons exploded from the gutters and circled the block. My mother turned away until her coughing seizure subsided. I stood there wondering why I didn't just run.

"As for your incomprehensible sister," she resumed hoarsely, "she is now having sexual relations with a black man with only one arm. I am appalled and offended."

"I didn't know Teresa knew a black man with one arm."

"What do his arms have to do with anything? He *is* black!"

"*You* brought up his arms, Mother."

"The entire town has seen my daughter and a one-armed black man enter the Motor Lodge Motel every Wednesday afternoon for the purpose of sexual relations!"

I pretended to study the framework of the new stairway.

"Then there is your grandmother, who needs professional care and is systematically destroying my household." My mother extracted a sheet of paper from her robe. "I must live with this woman, dear. I'm sure you can imagine how depressing life has become, how unendurable."

On the sheet, written in my grandmother's hand, was the following catalog:

Help Teresie bathe
Change linens

Fix a nice breakfast for everybody
Try to make
Take a nap
Watch TV
Kill flies
Prepare a nice lunch for everybody
Clean potatoes and beets
Feed the birds
Try to make
Call Mrs. Fischgrund
Walk down the block and back
Prepare a nice dinner for everybody
Kill flies
Watch the stars
Help Teresie undress
Try to sleep

I returned the sheet. "I have never," my mother said, "been more depressed by anything in my entire life. At least at a rest home she'd be surrounded by other useless people. I hope you see my point, dear."

"Actually," I said gently, "I don't."

"Oh, I suppose I've been more depressed once or twice. Certainly the day Teresa was crippled in that godforsaken little car which I warned her about, or the night my son came into his mother's house unspeakably drunk and excoriated her and his defenseless grandmother and sister like a wild lunatic, blaming every one of us for his decision not to marry Leah Summit."

"My family's got nothing to do with Leah Summit and me."

"But you said that your father and I had such a poisonous relationship that you just counted your lucky stars you still liked girls."

"I was drunk, Mother."

"Indeed, you were drunk."

"I'm sorry if I offended you."

"No, I'm afraid you undoubtedly meant what you said, dear. Because you were crying and screaming like a madman."

I looked away. "Why can't you remember all the good things that have occurred between us, Mother?" I was grabbing at straws and we both knew it.

"Because I'm terribly afraid that the good which has existed between us is superficial in comparison to the irremediably disastrous. You see, dear, my family has destroyed my capacity for feeling."

I breathed deeply several times. "With all due respect," I said, "I recommend you quadruple your Valium intake."

My mother was musing into space—lost to us, probably, forever.

"I took Valium just once, several years ago. It didn't agree with me. I stood in a corner, frightened to death, while your father screamed for his lunch."

"You could," I said, "smoke hashish and snap amyl nitrate. You could sit on the beach high as the sky and lose yourself in loud music. You could do codeine and Quaaludes and smoke marijuana and drink vodka and grapefruit juice and stare at your big toe all day. In short, Mother, you could find ways of filling in time in uncreative and self-destructive ways that would surely be an improvement on your present condition."

My mother, nonplussed, blinked at me with exquisite contempt. "That little outburst reflects, I'm afraid, the absolute depravity of your cynically abject generation. I simply cannot tell you how profoundly sorrowful you have made me feel for my children's children and my children's children's children."

She stared at me, extinguished her cigarette and raised her hand to her forehead.

"I really must try to nap before dinner, dear. You've given

me a terrible migraine. Try not to forget that message to your father."

THE BOARDWALK IS MORE SUPPLE THAN CONCRETE. THE RUN from Bradley to Spring Lake is five miles. My strategy required a month of ten-mile days, and then two weeks of fifteen-mile days. By winning the marathon, I would redeem a lost past, win my girl's heart and astonish a community of skeptics who harbored a silent but tangible belief that my capacity for success was limited to failure.

The tag of my jockstrap read 26–32 SMALL. I looked down at myself in the cottage, thought "average" a more appropriate rubric and composed a mental letter to the BVD people while dressing. Thereafter I jogged to the boardwalk to perform my stretching exercises.

When I came up from touching my toes, I saw Eliot Howard. He was waiting beside the snack stand in white jogging shorts, tortoiseshell sunglasses and a blue T-shirt that featured an orange sun and, beneath it in white, the words NO NUKES. He rose from a wooden chair to shake my hand.

"Dennis."

"Eliot."

"I've brought this for you." He nodded to the chair. "It's a Colonial oak I've relacquered and recaned. I do hope you like it."

"Look," I said. "We're just running together. I don't want chairs or flowers or chocolates every time we meet."

"It took me quite a while to refinish it, actually. I've been living in a motel for two months and just opened my store. I have a nice bookshelf, handmade, if you would prefer that."

The man's earnestness bespoke instability. Nonetheless, I accepted the gift on behalf of Leah's manuscript and ass.

"It's not really a gift, Dennis. Frankly, I anticipate that people will admire it and then ask where you purchased it. You'll tell them my store."

The chair had four legs, but I suggested to Eliot that it would have difficulty keeping pace with us. He carried the antique to the beach guard's entrance stand, where an octogenarian retiree in a safari hat—hired every summer to enforce payment upon the citizenry—agreed to watch it for us.

We ran past a miniature golf course; a pinball arcade blasting the Boss, Springsteen, from a jukebox; a Snocone gallery encircled by a herd of day-camp troublemakers; and finally, a concourse of Syrian delinquents flipping baseball cards for loose joints.

Removing his shirt while running, Eliot Howard said, "I've been a runner since Kennedy was murdered. I started in law school to keep from smoking and to please my ex-wife, who left me last year for a twenty-one-year-old student of hers. Our son will be fifteen this fall. After my wife left me, I quit my law practice and suffered a series of nervous breakdowns. That's about the only time I haven't run in close to twenty years. Do you mind if I talk?"

"Talk-ho," I said.

We ran on, the Atlantic to our left, the sun to our right, the wind blowing hotly into us from the south.

"I was married when I was twenty-four. I don't really know how to live without a woman. Do you mind if I ask your age?"

I stared straight ahead, my mind beginning to empty from the running, and owned up.

"That's how old I was when our Teddy was born. He doesn't believe in marriage. Manhattan kids aren't like kids anywhere else. When Teddy was fourteen he announced that he was a practicing bisexual. What are you?"

"Resolutely troubled, Eliot."

We must have done a mile before Eliot Howard spoke again.

"For a long time I was like you are now. I didn't understand why I was unhappy. I mean, really, Dennis, how can you know what you need to make you happy if you don't know who you are? Am I boring you with this?"

"I don't mind," I said.

"One day I was running on the grounds of the sanitarium. Suddenly I comprehended the horrible truth that at thirty-eight I had no Self, just a face with which to face other faces. Am I making myself clear?"

"I'm listening," I said, breathless from the pace he was setting.

"Well, I'm afraid the breakdown was the first truly authentic act I ever committed. Admittedly, it's rather terrifying at first to realize how different you are from who everyone told you you were supposed to be; but then it's wonderful. Accepting yourself—your real Self—is finding God, Dennis, believe me."

When we had finished the run and were drinking at the fountain, Eliot Howard said, "Of course, maybe I feel this renewal of confidence because I've just opened a store and met a sensitive and beautiful woman. She works as a waitress at a local bar where I drink, but she's working on a book and has a publisher for it. But hell, you're probably sick of listening to me. I think I'll run this mania out of me. Hope I'll see you tomorrow."

He turned and shot away so suddenly that I had no chance to raise his wooden gift above my head and bash his brains out with it.

IT WAS LATE ENOUGH IN THE AFTERNOON THAT, ASIDE FROM the sea gulls, only those who had fallen asleep were left on the beach. Dennis was there, for example, curled against a young lady in the bottom half of a black bikini. A book lay on her stomach in the shape of a pup tent.

She opened her eyes. "Help you, soldier?"

"Name's Tramp Bottoms. That's my dog resting his nose on your exposed left nipple. Where'd you go this morning?"

"Secret."

When I sat down I said, "I wonder if you'd be interested in having dinner with me tonight. My treat."

"Tonight's impossible."

"Mind if I ask why?"

"Date."

"Date? With whom?"

"A man, I believe."

I fell into shock. I covered my eyes and prayed for the past to come back. "I'll never speak with you again," I whispered.

She closed her eyes. "I'm sleeping now, Tramp, deeply sleeping, so I can't hear you anymore."

I watched her beautiful face for a long time. She didn't once peek. Finally I hid my head in her shoulder and closed my eyes. She stroked my hair. I heard the ocean crashing and the late-afternoon wind moving over us.

"It's all your fault," she said gently. "I've thought about it a lot. Marriage isn't the issue. The issue is that I can't help you anymore because you won't let me; it seems to mortify you. I mean, how can you say you love a person when you won't accept their help?"

I didn't say anything; you can't commiserate with the successful unless you are one of them.

I walked north along the sea for a long while, Dennis at my side. On the way home—that is, *on the way back;* to what, I can't say—I spotted my illustrious father feeding Wonderbread to the sea gulls.

"Mom's depressed and hinting at suicide again," I told him.

The birds were all over him, his shoulders and head, with dozens at his feet. "There's nothing I can do about that, Junior. I married a witch and can't control the destinations of her broomstick."

"Why don't you get serious!"

"Never worked for me."

I turned to the ocean. Dennis was riding a wave to shore, stick in mouth. "I suggest you put your toys and booze away and go back to her."

"I go back to her, Junior, and you'll have a complete set of parents talking suicide."

The carousel started twirling on the boardwalk and carnival music piped eerily into the slippage of afternoon.

"At least do something constructive," I said.

"That's a curious suggestion, coming from you. But I'll say this much. I filched the *Village Voice* from the cottage this morning and decided to place an ad in the personals section. Also answered two entreaties myself."

I turned back to him. "You're joking."

"You just said for me to get serious."

"You wrote an advertisement for the *Voice* announcing your needs?" I glanced down the beach at my fleeing credulity. "What exactly did you write to these women?"

"Wrote the truth: *'Cock-happy Pappy with bankrupt hideawee desires pinup girlie of lost youth for summer of fun and games.'* "

I turned away and walked back to where my troubles began. Leah, however, was gone. Once home, I phoned her immediately. Mrs. Summit was delighted to say, "Leah left this sec on a date in a convertible sportster. Who's this?"

"No one you'd want to know," I said, and depressed the phone's silver-colored cradle with my nose.

I WAS STAFFING THE MELODY OF "COASTLINE CRUCIFIXION" when I shot away from the piano in a marijuana burst of paranoia. By the look in my eyes in the bathroom mirror, one would have sworn that I had just seen the Father, Son and Holy Ghost gang-banging the Virgin herself in the Chapel of Love.

Around then something scratched at the door. Dennis had dragged a bloodstained bone the size of a horse leg to the back stoop. The fibula wouldn't fit through the doorframe, and my dog appealed to me with his irresistible brown eyes. But I refused assistance, anticipating one of the terrier's elaborate goofs.

Dennis is a sick dog, a merciless one. When I said "No!" he entered the kitchen, tail wagging, grabbed at the cuff of my pants and began yanking and shaking until he'd brought me to the floor. Then he ran outside again, dragging the skeleton.

A pamphlet from the Jehovah's Witnesses was tacked to the doorknob. The quotation on the *Watchtower* cover read, "A man's own folly wrecks his life, and then he bears a grudge against the Lord." They threatened to call again.

Sometimes there are presences in a house. It is difficult to explain. One simply senses that the Devil himself has invited six or eight of his most disreputable sycophants into your favorite room to fuck with your grieving mind.

I escaped to the yard for surcease.

The full moon was casting blue shadows. The leaves rattled. I'm dying, I thought, one second at a time while Leah is seeing another man. Well, Dennis was intent on burying his bone, and there seemed some connection. You do not stop Dennis, however, once his mind is made up. I watched the dirt fly. Then he popped his head above the excavation and began dragging in the bone. The burial bogged down when he tried to fit the bone's length into the trench's width; it was slightly pathetic. When I began to help him, he stared reprovingly at me, his nose and face covered with dirt. For a moment, before I backed off, I believe he was entertaining thoughts of *attack*. In the end he arranged the bone to his liking and returned the dirt to its hole.

I lay on the hammock and watched him sitting in the darkness above his investment. "Where's Leah?" I whispered. "Where's Leah?" He stood up and looked around frantically. I said, "On a date, Dennis. A goddamn date. Next time I see Eliot Howard I will ask you to kill him! Kill!"

He lifted his leg and marked his property, then ran off. I did, too, to Leah's. I peeked in her window and discovered her absence. I waited on the front stoop until three A.M., when I stormed home to compose "Betrayer."

THE DAILY ACCIDENT WAS IN FULL COMMERCIAL SWING WHEN I returned to the Summits' house to have it out. The house itself was easily the most immaculate tombstone of domestic heterosexual vacuity in town. The aluminum siding had me cursing the unimaginative expediency of synthetics. Mrs. Summit, my favorite, answered the door in a swimsuit, a beach chair dangling from her arm. Her hair was fluffed like silver cotton candy and her beauty marks had been darkened with eye pencil. Needless to say, a Viceroy dangled from her mouth.

"I have nothing this afternoon, Martin."

I looked behind me into emptiness before turning back to her. "Mrs. Summit?"

"Oh, my Lord, if it isn't you! But we seem so different with all that hairdo covering our face. Well, I guess we do look like a rock star even if we aren't to be one."

"I thought Leah might be home."

"Leah? Why no, hon. Our talented girl is just about the busiest little beaver I've ever seen."

"Determined to gang-bang me into repentance, you think?"

"Come again, hon?"

"I say, where is she now?"

"Well, for just a sec about half a minute ago she was here." Mrs. Summit looked around. "Oh yes, she went off with a man in a Cadillac."

I smiled my despair. "I'll let you get to the beach, Mrs. Summit."

"That's just fine, hon. Assuming we locate our Coppertone number two."

She found number two in the pink cotton handbag that was slung across her shoulder and locked the door. I felt the sun on my face as I walked away. Mrs. Summit called for me to "hold on one sec." I turned around.

"We all hear Whit's trying to sell that eyesore." She held on to the railing as she delicately descended the front steps in her high-heel beach shoes. "'Course, the place developed such a nasty reputation after the lice were found on those Latin cooks that me and Whart can't imagine who'd buy it out from under him. Well, everybody west of the beach is certainly watching to see whether he'll hold up or go under."

Mrs. Summit no sooner finished her Viceroy than she started another. In the process Mr. Summit emerged from the garage pushing a parade of gas-powered machinery. I counted a lawnmower, an edger, a trimmer and, naturally, a leaf blower. Wharton wore his work outfit: the stretch bathing suit, Marine cap and boots. He was rotting inside out and the manifold protrusion of bones informed my estimate of six months.

"He's been spitting blood all month and can't work!" Mrs. Summit seemed proud of the fact. "'Course he never could sit still more than one sec or two, and I don't think this cold's going to stop him."

Wharton Summit nodded his agreement. "I'm a workaholic from a better age and can't apologize for it—not knowing there's a nation of welfare beggars who my kind keep in groceries. Meantime, we're all waiting to see if you'll help out the family once the resort don't sell. Whit's worried off his rocker and I can't imagine there's an ounce of comfort for him, knowing his son's retired before ever knowing the value of a paycheck from the private sector."

I yawned. "Just takes one song, Mr. Summit."

"'Course the problem there, hon," Mrs. Summit said, "is how just about nearly everyone of your disposition never makes it and never knows when to quit. Personally, I feel about one hundred percent certain that Leah walked out on you vis-à-vis her wanting a nice future. Now, if you were, say, a professional individual with a place of business where you could count up a day's receipts, well then, Whart and me feel our girl might feel less inclined to be dating her head off."

I studied them, Mr. and Mrs. Summit, before waving goodbye to the most loathsome couple south of Iceland with the most desirable daughter north of Patagonia.

I STOOD ON THE SIDEWALK WITH MY BEACH TOWEL, DENNIS tugging at the other end. Grandma was killing flies on the screened section of the porch. Some of us realize this is murder. But even supposing a more ecumenical application of Love Thy Neighbor, there is the obvious problem of enforcement.

Grandma's raiment consisted of a swimsuit with attached skirt and my former grandfather's former golf hat.

"Mommy and me and Leah is going to the beach now. Leah's looking for a house with a real estate man that drives a Cadillac!"

"Leah's here?"

"Helping Mommy put on a bathing suit." Grandma leaned into the mesh screening and whispered, "Mommy's so fat this season she don't look herself no more. She started crying at the breakfast table. Leah don't look happy herself and neither do you." Grandma implored me with doleful eyes. "Why don't Sonny go inside right now and say he was wrong and learned his lesson and won't fight no more. Do it for Grandma!"

She was old. She was very old, with thin white hair. Sooner than later they would tuck her into a coffin and she would disappear into memory as swiftly as a dream.

"Grandma, I've been sitting in a chair climbing walls all night. Some other time."

Grandma maintained her whisper. "Leah told Mommy and me how you was the most talented person she ever knew and that we don't understand what makes you tick."

"She did?"

"She said she loved you so much she can't sleep no more at night and drives around with a man that had a nervous breakdown."

I stared down the block to the ocean and reviewed a number of assumptions. When I turned back, my mother and Leah stepped onto the porch. Seeing the two women in tandem was nothing less than chilling. Leah wore a plum-colored bathing suit I had bought her two years earlier. She had always been slinky and dark, and her widow's peak of black hair never failed to leave me afflicted with nympholeptic paralysis.

Grandma said to my mother, "Just look at how they look at one another," and slammed the swatter against the screen.

I set off around the house. I glanced back furtively and all three women were watching me. Leah was the only one to wink.

IV

STAGE FRIGHT SCRAMBLES YOUR BRAIN, RUINS YOUR VOICE AND paralyzes your fingers. Famous people have quit because of it. I am not one of them—of the famous people, I mean.

On the other hand, consuming a narcotic substance to combat stage fright disconnects your brain, frogs your voice and melts your fingers. My mean between extremes is the following prescription: two of your mother's five-milligram barbiturates with oolong tea and vodka one hour before gig time. Also, a pack of cigarettes and a pair of shades, the latter to obscure the tendency of the terrified eyes to glaze and splay in six·directions simultaneously.

I drove to Manhattan in the Avanti, my demo, *Rock Bottom,* blasting on the tape deck. The turnpike scares me. It is bounded by toxic waste dumps that blow up from time to time and by gasoline refineries whose smokestacks blast flames hundreds of feet into the noxious atmosphere. Just across the river is Manhattan, an island of detritus and crime that suggests promises it cannot keep. Draw around Manhattan a circle whose circumference is a hundred miles, and the only instance of redemption is Leah Summit.

Well, I sat in a darkened corner of the End with my prescription equanimity, observing a banjo act, a folk-song duet, a Fogelberg specimen in beard and flannel shirt poeticizing rivers and *"the good earth."* The good earth, indeed. Problem being, of course, that on a quotidian basis the good earth is as eternally lost to us as our lost youth.

A derivative New Wave ensemble à la Sex Pistols followed; enough noise and hate to fuel the hearts of the good earth's ubiquitous bad boys and girls. Owen Chance, the house manager and cheesecake prima donna, worked the mixing board and simultaneously gyrated his hips. For the most part the Stereo Types evoked the kind of sympathetic applause you don't want to follow. The band had obviously packed the place with a scummy retinue of groupies, not exactly my element. Those horizontally elongated green lenses in white frames leave me disquieted. Fortunately, most of the wastrel loyalists bopped off following the Types' final number, "Stick It."

When the lights came up for the stage clearing, Owen Chance—dressed in chic pink luminosity, white necklace and rose-tinted sunglasses—joined me in the corner. He offered me his left hand, palm down, and I shook it with my right hand. Manhattan, I thought, has become a clearinghouse of arcane ring, key, hankie and hand codes, languages more foreign than those of California and Babel.

"I want my guy's music to make everything we've heard tonight sound irrelevant."

"I hope," I said.

"I've saved you for very last for just this purpose." Owen stared at me. "You should wear eyeliner."

"Ha ha," I said, and lifted my guitar from its case.

"Will you be needing the piano?"

I nodded and Owen swished to the stage to reposition the Sohmer.

"I want my minstrel gigolo to go for it tonight!" he called, adjusting the voice mike. "One never knows who might stop in for a drink and hear guy doing his thing."

"Dig it, Owen."

"Just be groovy tonight, guy. Super groovy."

The tables surrounding the stage filled with the bar's overflow of summer-school aesthetes. It was a few minutes past eleven when Owen announced from the mixing board, "Please welcome *Mr. Tramp Bottoms.*"

I took my Gibson by the neck and moved through a greeting of indifference and clanging silverware. Naturally, the phone rang and a tray dropped. I said, "I wrote this running one step ahead of the Devil," and launched into "Rock Bottom," featuring a mellifluous alternation of major and minor chords to pull at the nation's archetypal heartstrings.

I've gone my whole life
Gotten nowhere
Probably nowhere to go
But does that mean
I'm supposed to be happy
Being a means to
No end

Maybe there's no object
For our desire
And what we do desire
Is not what we should
But I'm not happy
Being a means to
No end
How can you be so mean to me
When you know I'm going to end

Once I thought living for you
Was my only escape and
The only desirable thing
But sometimes I wonder about love
If it's only a way of disguising
Our cold and our separate end

Yeah, the earth's going to melt down
Entropy will take us each
Centers never do hold
But we can
Use our empty arms
To bring us peace from harm
We'll fade away together

No, I'm not happy being
A means to no end
We shouldn't be mean
While we're together
We need to remember
There's an end to forever

There was the requisite applause as I switched to the guitar
and sang my LA introspective number, "Entranced."

What is it I want to come true?
Baby, there's nothing on earth that's new
And I've seen it all
For a little love
There's always a lot of hate

No wonder I'm scared
No wonder I'm so sad
No wonder I'm black and blue

What I need is a place to hang
Up my hang-ups
Hang onto you
'Cause we break up
And I break down

There's no big task
No need to run so fast
What's the point
When you only sink deeper
Into your messed-up head?

Hey, without you
I'll be a wondering Jew
Go from one bad bed to the next
What I need is a place to hang
Up my hang-ups
                     Hang onto you

No wonder I'm scared
So black and blue
So sad without you

There was applause. Owen switched the spot from blue to crimson and tracked me back to the piano. I remembered the way they once screamed for Rundgren to "go all night! Go all night!" and sang "Hard Drugs." Afterward I stared through the smoky spots at the audience and sang "Crazy for Free."

At my finish Owen said, "Mr. Tramp Bottoms!" I blew the audience a kiss before returning to my table in the darkened corner to hold hands with anticlimax.

A waitress wondered if I'd like a drink.

"You enjoy my music?"

"When did you play?"

"Arsenic on the rocks, please."

"I've been very busy."

I watched her walk away. Owen sat down across from me. "May I speak candidly, guy?" He lit a cigarette and placed his chin in his hands. Smoke streamed from his nose.

"Shoot."

"I am many kinky things, guy, but I'm no shootist. And fist-fucking in my book is the worst kind of cruelty to animals."

I was thinking, I can't make it another day without Leah, when Owen said, "Two of the numbers are positively fabulous. The others are nicely supportive—nothing more, nothing less."

"Let's talk endlessly about the two fabulous ones."

" 'Brain-Damaged Heart' and 'Entranced,' with full rock-band support, could make you the nation's sweetheart."

"Don't stop," I said.

"They're well-balanced, they're intelligently and accessibly lyrical. They prove to me you're an enormously talented kid in need of a band to distinguish you from lots of other very talented kids."

The waitress returned; we ordered alcohol.

"What I propose," Owen said, "is that I manage you for six months on a strictly verbal-agreement basis. I want you to think about it."

I did. "Why do you want to?"

Owen smoothed his eyebrows and set his face in his hands. "In the first place, next to money and sexual gratification, in that order, music is the most important thing in my life. It keeps me from feeling dead, which I assume is what living is supposed to be all about. Secondly, every record company on earth is searching for a boy with a hit single, and I think you have one for them."

Our drinks came. Owen immediately ordered two more of the same.

"Listen," I confessed, "I've been submitting demos for years."

"Of course you have, guy. You and sixty thousand other rock 'n' roll neophytic dopes. And to whom have we submitted these demos? To low-level nameless railheads with no clout and an office at the wrong end of the musical hallway." Owen washed down a pill with his wine. "I have contacts all over town, guy. I've reviewed for *Creem* and *Circus* for ages. I know people. I can be ingratiating. But with class. And clout. I have my ways. I know the ins and outs of the industry. Also, I'm not above being an animal, a cruel one if I must be, and every good manager must be willing to do an animal act for his guy's sake."

The bar vodka, without the oolong tea, went down as smoothly as battery acid.

"You've managed before, then?" I asked hoarsely.

"Just once. My wife. She caught on as a model and quit the club scene. But I got her dates, put her in touch."

"Your wife?" I sounded more incredulous than I would have liked.

"Torrey and I operate a very open marriage, guy. I'd classify it as a psychological addiction. She's at the bar." Owen pointed her out. "She thinks you're marvelous."

"A nation of *fan.*"

"You shall have fans, guy. Heaps of them. I sense it happening to you. Fairy tales can come true. Owen can make them happen for you."

I asked for specifics.

"Everything, guy. I will produce high-quality demos in reputable sound studios where I have ins. I will pander said demos in the inner sanctums of the crass world of record-company profiteers. I will arrange club dates all over town for guy so that he can concentrate exclusively on his lyrics and melodies. In a word, guy, Owen will be your commercial agent in this stinking world of mercenary designs. Do you begin to see the scenario for inevitable success coming into focus?"

I nodded. Owen lit a cigarette.

"What's the financial angle?" I asked.

"No angle, guy. Only the traditional and mutual cuts for our different and singular talents. I'm a super manager asking for twenty-five percent of the take, plus expenses. We sink instead of swim, I swallow the cost. All I require of you is promo photographs, that you get your bod into town for rehearsals and recordings when I say so, and that you sit down with me sometime ultra soon and review everything you've ever composed." Owen exhaled smoke from his nose. "That's my proposition, guy. Take it or leave it, but don't disbelieve it."

I was too ambitious with the drink and coughed on his arm. "Let me think about it," I said.

Owen rose. "Incidentally, my wife thinks you are very hot stuff." He went off to the bar.

She appeared without him, introduced herself and explained that Owen was occupied in the men's, "sampling drug." Her sunglasses were shaped like two hearts, and she wore a burgundy dress with a black belt. She sat across from me, sipping a drink through a straw.

"Your eyes lit up just now when you saw me," she said.

"Did they?"

"You bet, mister."

"But I'm wearing shades," I said.

"Hey, you turn me on like a radio."

I observed her lipstick staining the tip of the straw; I smiled.

"Lust at first sight, mister."

Well, I stared into my drink, wondering if I had the change to phone Leah. You could hear the barbiturates in Torrey's voice. When I looked up, Owen's better, or other, half was observing herself in a hand mirror. "Why am I beautiful? Can you tell me? Do you know?"

I sat there, clearly stumped, counting coins in my hand.

"Because if I were ugly, mister, I'd kill myself." She turned the mirror to me and held it a foot from my nose. "If you were me, would you fuck a man with that face?"

Observing myself, I thought, if Leah were with me, this would never have happened. Torrey said, "I would if I were you," and I wondered if she were circuitously telling me to go do it to myself.

"I knew someone just like you once," she said. "He overdosed last winter. Twenty-one years old. May I ask you something?"

I wanted to be home in a sunlit room with Dennis, the smell of lilacs all about and God's angels blowing bubbles on the wings of returning faith. "I've got to make a phone call," I said.

"You love me. I can tell you love me."

"Of course."

"Of course you don't, you mean."

"Of course."

"So why should I want to fuck you?"

"I'll make this call and be right back." I stood up.

She held my hand in hers. "Because I loved him, mister. He was a magician."

"I'm no magician."

"A magician with drug. He'd put it on my clit and french it off. I'd die every time and he'd bring me back to life. The boy was God. Then he died. Now you must be him for me."

Owen returned to the table.

Torrey said abruptly, "I'm a feminist with bisexual quirks. I'm tired of dealing with white men!" and left the table.

I grabbed my guitar and shook Owen's hand good-bye. He

proffered me his card and told me to call him the next day.

"Music," he said, "is life. And life is business. I'll manage the business if you'll do the music. As for your life, I'm not responsible."

"We'll speak," I said.

I phoned Leah from a corner pay phone amid a parade of androgynous punkers and glittering New Wave groupies. Mrs. Summit answered as warmly as an ice pick.

"Mrs. Summit," I shouted, a finger in my ear, "this is Tramp Bottoms. I'm calling long distance from a street phone to speak with Leah."

"That's the sort of politeness we all expected from you about a year or more ago."

"Mrs. Summit, I hold no special animus toward you. I want you to know that. Please put Leah on."

"Hon, your vocab must be twice the size of your wallet. I never do know what you are talking about and just wish you were the sort of man who could buy my daughter and her family nice big dinners in restaurants instead of serving up a steady diet of cheekiness that nobody wants to hear."

"Mrs. Summit," I shouted, "would you please put Leah on the phone!"

"How can I, hon, when she's out with her new boyfriend, who's got a wallet full of credit cards!"

"Mrs. Summit?"

I heard the hang-up hum resonate in my ear and left the phone to dillydally on its silver-colored cable in the booth's fluorescence. I was a nice person, essentially. I wouldn't hurt a *soul* for anything. Still, speeding toward home on the New Jersey Turnpike, when I prayed for God to shine his mercy on Mrs. Summit, I didn't mean this to suggest that I was not eager for her less eternal self to find an immediate and painful return to forever.

DENNIS KISSED ME HELLO AT THE DOOR OF THE COTTAGE.
I poured him a glass of cognac and demonstrated with more
than three glasses how to drink the stuff. Then I took the
terrier for a walk in the moonlight. Somehow, we were soon
standing in front of Leah Summit's lighted window. Looking
in, I could see her feet under the covers.

"Leah?"

Her feet didn't move. I raised the screen and climbed in.
When Mrs. Summit, dozing in her curlers, a book on her chest,
spotted me stepping into the room, she bolted up and
screamed her fucking head off.

Mr. Summit appeared at the door with a military handgun
and meat cleaver. I had my hands above my head to indicate
my surrender. "Leah said I could."

Mr. Summit stood within the doorframe, his member hanging through the unsnapped fly of his pajamas. "Leah's moved
out on us!"

I backed toward the window, eying the pistol. "This won't
happen again, sir."

"If it was to, son, I swear to Christ I'd shoot. The Constitu-
tion says I got the right to blow apart citizens who break and
enter."

I stepped out into the darkness. Dennis stood there with a
stick in his mouth, wagging his tail at my appearance.

I walked home behind him, through backyard flower beds
and broken fence posts. I was in Leah's doghouse, and Dennis
knew of paths between her place and mine that I'd never
dreamed of. I was willing to try anything.

V

THE NEXT MORNING I STOOD MESMERIZED ABOVE A SEWER grate wondering whether or not I should work with Owen Chance. When I had the answer, I looked up and spotted my father standing on the retaining wall of Shark River inlet, addressing a lineup of hometown delinquents who listened attentively behind separate piles of rocks. A model clipper ship tossed twenty yards offshore in the backwater froth. It was hot, windless, and my father, completing his instructions, staggered momentarily while bending for his radio transmitter. Directly the clipper ship sailed away in a close-hauled tack, SSE, and my father, unregal from booze, announced, "Fire at will!"

Around the time he cried "One more minute!" a flat rock, expertly hurled, curved into the mainsail and snapped the clipper's boom. There was a momentary cheer from the peanut gallery, and my father, astonished by the hit, dropped the transmitter. Thereupon his craft became little better than the proverbial sitting duck, and the big kid at the line's end lofted half a brick in a bull's-eye parabola that smashed the starboard bow. The little ship disappeared for good to the applause of the puberty-crazed canaille.

I approached my father from the blind side. He was kneeling beside a cigar box with his proposition—50¢ ENTRANCE FEE, POSITIVELY NO CREDIT!—taped to the open lid. The children gathered at shore, watching for signs of flotsam.

"So," I said, "drunk again."

He craned his neck to see me. "Drunk," he replied, "doesn't matter so much as what sort of deeds you perform *while drunk.*"

"May I ask what you call your little performance here?"

"Call it? I call it making a summer day a whole lot better for potential hoodlums here in our stale slice of hometown USA." He transferred the change from the cigar box to his pocket.

"Your own small corner of the private sector, I presume."

"No, Junior. No money in the ships. I make quite a bit with the planes, but nothing on the ships. They can't hit my miniature Spitfires, though they love like hell trying. They'll remember me as a crazy fool when they're older, but right now they're having as much fun as broom-handling streetlights. I consider this my community service."

"That's fine," I said. "But must you always be drunk three steps over the line of respectability before you offer your services?"

"Sadness, Junior."

"Answer my question."

"Last damn thing your commander wants is respectability. Tree-lined streets all across America are housed with respectable citizens, and it's about the saddest thing this man has ever set his eyes upon."

My father cleared his throat and turned to the water. "When I don't drink, Junior, the day stays at ten-fifteen A.M. for three weeks. Seven sober hours feel like a lifetime."

"Daddy," I said, not without grief, "you are the rock of

secular strength doing a very bad imitation of Silly Putty. I think it's time we had a serious talk. Wreck to wreck."

He put his big hand on my shoulder. "Marvelous, Junior. Splendid. What say we drag our bottoms to the Pour House and get ourselves etherized like patients upon a table."

"Goddamn you, I'm serious."

"Fault of youth. That too shall pass."

"Be at the cottage for dinner tonight at seven. Spaghetti okay?"

"Splendid once again, Junior. Spaghetti's my favorite. I shall bring us a nice burgundy. Some Indonesian coffee." He smiled at me, swaying slightly. "Just consider it, Junior: Whit Bottoms and his son Aldo Huxley eating dinner together after all these years." He looked at the children swimming in the water, collecting wreckage. "I'd live my entire life over again to have dinner with my boy tonight."

I HAD CUT AND HAMMERED THE LAST THREE STEPS OF THE front stairs when I noticed a little shadow peeking over my shoulder.

"Well, well, Midas Muffler!"

"Merrill Miller!"

"What's cooking, Mickey Mantle?"

"My father says I shouldn't talk to you. He says your father's a fatso dumbbell and an offshore idiot."

"Well, Mickey Mouse, your father blows donkey dicks!"

"You just cursed at me!"

"So?"

"You know what?"

"Tell me."

"Cunt fuck shit you!"

Grandma stepped outside in time to spot Merrill Miller

running toward the sound of fire trucks speeding down the street. She stood there, stupefied, holding a tray of brownies and milk.

"I'd've sworn that was Marcey Miller's little boy, Merrill."

I shrugged, sawing: Vera Bottoms' little boy.

"I can't imagine why he'd run off, Sonny. He comes to Grandma's for brownies and milk every day at two-thirty."

I savored every bit of Merrill Miller's two brownies and decided to repair to the Atlantic. I returned to the cottage for my wet-suit top and surfboard. Strangely enough, when I arrived, Merrill Miller was standing next to my mother beside the fire engines, watching the cottage burn to the ground.

My mother affected the chilly manner of a closet neurotic miles from her Valium cache. "The fire chief says someone neglected to extinguish a flame beneath a coffeepot. I'm just so furious with you that I'm afraid I cannot remain in your presence a moment longer."

"I cannot believe this is happening, Mother."

"I'm afraid this has nothing to do with categories of belief, dear. The fact is that the cottage I entrusted to you is irreparably damaged."

I watched columns of black smoke dissolve through the trees into the sky. The sound of the hoses made me want to go myself. "Don't cry, Mother."

She turned her shoulder from me and blew her nose. "You'll be staying in the attic now, dear," she said, sniffing. "But I want Dennis to stay in the basement so that the house is not overrun with fleas and vermin. And you must promise me that you'll stay out of my kitchen, away from all appliances and electric sockets."

"I'm certain arson is involved here, Mother."

"I'd much rather believe that you burned it down by accident, dear." Despite the flow of tears, she did manage a tragic smile. "In either case, I'm afraid I simply can no longer bear to remain near you."

I watched her walk down the street and turn the corner. Merrill Miller, meanwhile, had taken to throwing rocks at the cottage's front windows. James Tunnel, the policeman, restrained him with a look.

I LAY ON THE SURFBOARD FACING SHORE. THE FIVE O'CLOCK SUN glowed in the windows of the family's attic—my most recent asylum. The joint burned my finger and I snapped off the head. I closed my eyes and told myself I would reunite with Leah Summit and redeem my ignominious reputation by establishing my own republic of rock 'n' roll fans by twenty-six. This fantasy was fast escorting me toward equanimity when something brushed my thigh. My breathing caught and a headline crossed my mind in ticker-tape staccato: SHARK . . . EATS . . . FAILURE! When I felt the brushing again, I screamed and commenced desperate thrashing. Something passed beneath the board and the next thing I knew my wrist and ankle had been seized. Then a fat man equipped with a black snorkel and mask surfaced beside me.

"You have succeeded in scaring the shit out of me!"

He raised his mask. "How many times have I warned you not to swim alone?"

"I'm twenty-five years old!"

"Next time I catch you out here alone, I'll bite off a big toe."

"You need professional help!"

"Barber told me the same thing. Gave me the names of two broads for hire. Naturally, this is confidential."

"Don't clear your goddamn nose here!"

"Stop screaming at your father."

"Fuck you!"

Floating on his back, hands behind his head, my father said, "When a son of mine can't take a joke and leaves a girl like Leah Summit, he just can't be the one to talk to me about mental problems."

"Leave me alone."

"Incidentally, just came from the cottage, where I planned to chill the wine, and discovered you've left us with a pile of ashes."

I put my hands to my ears.

"That cottage was never anything to me but one room of repairs after another. I'd be a liar if I didn't encourage you to do the same with the big house."

I lay with my stomach to the board and closed my eyes. I remembered how Leah Summit and I would get into bed on Saturday afternoons when it rained. I would lie there afterward, the windows open, listening to Pharaoh Sanders while Leah slept, her head generally on my chest, her hand between my legs.

"Junior?"

"Go away," I muttered, my eyes still closed. "You're a sick man. A mental patient."

"Means nothing today, Junior. All adults are mental patients. Little else to do as an adult."

"I'd stick with your barbershop queens and leave your son out of your life."

I paddled away from him toward the horizon. I got to my knees and looked for a wave. A catamaran was running free to the south. I could tell from the ponytail that one of the two sailors was Leah Summit.

I timed the swell imperfectly and washed ashore several yards behind my board. I was kneading sand from my suit, coughing up water, when I noticed my father waiting on the beach. His jockey shorts were transparent from the salt-water soaking, and he stepped from them without giving his whereabouts a second thought.

"What if it got around, "I said, scanning the beach, "that the owner of the Last Resort was spotted standing naked, scratching his member on the strand?"

He stepped into his Bermudas. "Place is up for sale. I could use the publicity." He lit a cigar and sent smoke into the sky. "Junior, in conclusion, Daddy quits!"

I said, "You never even tried," and walked toward the day's sunburst finish.

MY EMERGENCE FROM THE OAK TREE'S SHADOWS COINCIDED with Leah's emergence from the convertible. Leah said, "This is my brother, Tramp," and took my arm at the elbow. "Tramp, Eliot Howard."

Eliot was smiling; his arm extended winsomely across the death seat's headrest. He was tan and needed a shave.

"Talk about a coincidence!" he said.

I winked at the cuckolder and put my arm unbrotherly around Leah's waist.

A green sticker, pinned to the Fiat's visor, read, MENTAL HEALTH CLINIC PARKING PERMIT. The man's proclaimed instability, however, bothered me less than his good looks, which were redolent of an inveterate patricianism.

"Listen," Eliot said, "I do apologize for missing our run today, but you haven't shown up the last few times, so I invited Leah to go sailing. Perhaps you'd like to join us the next time?"

Leah could see it in my eyes. "We've got to go inside now, Eliot. I had a very nice time." She took me by the arm.

"I do hope," Eliot called, "that you didn't mind me revealing my affection for you today?"

"I'm glad you did," Leah answered.

"Would you like to get together tomorrow? I mean, would tomorrow be a good day for you?"

"Call her," I said. "She's bashful about making dates in front of me."

Eliot Howard waved to Leah as he pulled out, and I looked at her, at my sweat shirt, which terminated evocatively at mid-thigh. In addition there was the rest of her coppery legs down to the paisley-cloth high heels; and then her black hair and general beauty—sufficiently captivating to own any heart she wanted. She was my gypsy dream queen from way back, and my regret showed when she set her gray eyes on mine.

"We lived by a lake for six years and never once sailed," she said.

I stepped into her. "I'm scared of water," I said, and put my forehead against her shoulder.

"You are scared of anything with depth, sweetie."

"I'm scared of anyone who's crazy enough to love me."

"Shut up," she said kindly.

We stared at each other.

"You look so handsome with a tan," she said.

"Also, I'm an incurable depressive who is all alone inside his head."

"Try being more mysterious, Tramp."

"Is Eliot gay, I hope?"

"No. Now listen to me—"

"He looked like maybe he was, that maybe a good jilting could drive him to it. It's a shame, seeing as how Dennis and I will now have to kill him."

"Can you hear me?" My eyes were closed again, my head bowed, and Leah was speaking into my ear.

"Yes?"

"I am giving you twenty seconds to begin acting like the wonderful man you can be."

"I'm in pain, Leah. I've failed myself and I've failed you."

She'd undoubtedly had enough. Before the front door slammed, she called back, "It's known as adulthood. Look it up!"

I did.

adult (ə dult', ad'ult) adj. [L. *adultus,* pp. of *adolescere;* see ADO-LESCENT], ... n. 1. a mature person; man or woman. 2. an animal or plant that is grown up. 3. in *law,* a person who has come of age. —SYN. see **ripe**

ripe (rīp) adj. [ME.; AS.; akin to G. *reif;* for IE. base see RIP, v.], 1. . . . . . fully grown or developed, as animals ready to be slaughtered for food. . . . 6. ready to do, receive, or undergo something; fully prepared: as, *ripe* for trouble. 7. ready for some operation, treatment, or process. 8. ready to open or be lanced, as a boil. 9. sufficiently advanced; far enough along (*for* some purpose): said of time.

I wanted nothing to do with it.

VI

IN THE FORMATIVE YEARS OF MY RUINATION, I TENDED TO ROAM
the boardwalk with my sister. Most often it was after dinner
in the warm seasons. She'd push her doll carriage and I'd strap
on my Texas John Slaughter cap guns to protect her and the
kid. Some years later I would carry a quart bottle of beer in a
brown bag and my guitar, and she would bring a book to read,
usually a collection of Russian short stories, lent to her by her
girl friend up the street, Leah something-or-other. We'd sit on
a bench, the ocean rolling in before us, until dark. Sometimes
she'd read to me while I drank the beer, and sometimes I'd sing
for her after it was too dark to read. She, too, loved Rundgren.
During the summer of '72 I must have played "It Wouldn't
Have Made Any Difference" every night until the frost hit.

Teresa met Scotty that summer. He walked by the boards,
heard me playing "You Are My Window," said, "I'm a main-
liner myself. Todd is God in Philly," and sat down to listen.
It was the summer before our senior year in high school. Scotty
and Teresa wound up at Boston University and stayed together
until Scotty lost control of the wheel.

Strolling the boardwalk seven summers later, I was contemplating how the wheelchair might be indirectly my fault. This gave me an ache behind both eyes. When they focused after my rubbing, I saw Teresa sitting in her metal chair beside our favorite bench. The synchronicity left me searching the sky for God's marionette strings.

The moment my shadow eclipsed her, my sister turned to me, smiling, her eyes wrinkling in the corners. She had been reading a book, Lewis' *Joyful Christian;* we didn't need any of that.

"Do Myrna Loy for me," I said strategically.

She did my favorite part from *Mr. Blandings Builds His Dream House.* Naturally, I got to thinking about Leah Summit's rumored dream house and how Eliot Howard threatened to make it my nightmare. I hid my face in my hands. Teresa pulled my fingers apart and wondered if something was wrong.

"Nothing important," I said. "Only my life."

My serious sister frowned. "You'll probably be gratified to learn that I've come to the horrible conclusion that Jesus Christ lived and was crucified and died, but couldn't possibly have risen from the dead after three days."

I gazed over the medium purported to have once supported the little lamb. "He lacked a sense of humor," I said. "He never laughed, never even cracked a smile. One time he wept. Stan Laurel, on the other hand . . ."

Teresa turned away, mortified, and picked at her nails. "They say he never blinked his eyes or left footprints. I wanted so much to believe in him. But I just can't. I feel so lonesome again. I think I'm going to cry."

"You can't cry!" I kneeled beside her wheelchair and put my arm around her. I whispered, "I've come to save you through laughter."

She turned her face into my chest. "Funny," she said softly, "how an idea can keep you company when nothing else can. When the idea dies it's almost worse than a person dying."

I brushed her hair from her face. "The worst thing is when your dog dies. Thank God Dennis is immortal."

Well, she smiled. "Do something to cheer me up."

"Headstand?"

"Much dumber than that."

I thought a moment. "Put your arms around my neck."

After she obeyed, I lifted her from the wheelchair and walked down the wooden steps to the beach.

"What are you doing?"

"Something very dumb."

"Put me down."

"Not on your life, Mrs. B."

First the sand felt wet and firm beneath me and then the waves hit me at the knees. I jumped up. Teresa screamed, "Dumb, not crazy!"

I said, "Hold your breath," and clutching her tightly, kneeled to let the wave's crashing break over us. When we surfaced, Teresa's hair was straight and flat against her face, and she was gasping from the cold water. She cried, "I'm swimming. Swimming!" and was promptly washed away by a wave. I hurried over and, hugging her to me, returned to the shore.

We sat down in the wet sand; Teresa in my lap, her white dress transparent from the water. She let go of my neck and lay back, her face to the sun, her eyes closed.

"You're sillier than Erik Satie," she said.

I looked down the coast, counted to ten and thought, what the hell. "Grandma says you stay in your room all night and read books."

My sister opened her eyes. "What does Grandma want me to do—go out dancing?"

"That's no reason not to go out at all."

"I do go out. I work with children all day."

"I guess," I said, "what we're talking about is love."

"I love the children very much."

"Not that kind of love, Teresa."

She sat up on her elbows, breasts showing through the wet dress. "I'm afraid there's something about a wheelchair that takes that kind of love away from you."

A starfish came floating up in the surf. It was orange on top and white on the bottom. The white part was full of bristles, which moved with life. I twirled it into the water.

"Once," I said, "you were the life of the party."

She turned away, then appealed to me with her somber brown eyes. "Let's go back now." She drapped her arms around my neck; I lifted her gently and started up the beach.

"What about this one-armed man?" I said, our eyes not meeting.

"Carver? He drives the children to and from school."

"Mommy tells me she's seen you go into a motel with him."

"No doubt she has. Every Wednesday we have a Bible class."

"Did you know she thinks you go there to sleep with him?"

My sister frowned. "That's rather funny, considering that Carver is a Christian and a celibate." She paused to rub her nose against my shoulder. "Although I suppose being celibate and not a Christian is far funnier."

Neither of us, however, laughed.

Halfway up the steps, I said, "Want another ice-cold swim?" My sister confessed she'd prefer a hot bath, a dry dress, underpants without sand in the crotch and a push to work.

I did what I could.

MAYBE I WAS LOOKING FOR LEAH AND ELIOT, AND MAYBE I wasn't.

The tide was low. The gulls were scavenging. I thought, she is intent upon fixing my wagon; and probably will.

I was walking, as I am inclined to do, with my esteemless head down, my hands thrust in my cutoffs, kicking the water and thinking of new chords for "Coastline Crucifixion" when I noticed two girls waiting for me.

The redhead said, "God, you're Peter Frampton, right?"

"Tramp Bottoms."

"Who?"

I broke the two names into three syllables for them.

"You play for America, right?" asked the one in the white mesh suit.

"I hate America!"

"The group?"

"I hate America!"

"So you're no one famous?"

"Tramp Bottoms!"

"Well, we'd give anything to fuck Mick Jagger. Wouldn't you?"

"What?"

"You know, the *Stones. Jagger!*"

"How old are you two?"

"Twenty-six," the redhead said. "Combined."

MY FAVORITE SPOT ON THE JETTY WAS OCCUPIED. DENNIS WAS there with his goddamn horse bone. Also, a slinky woman with long black hair. And another person beside her, a man who, I suspected, owned a sports car. I'll say this much for Leah: She had her top in place. Eliot Howard had everything in place too, notwithstanding his emotions. He was wearing mirror shades; a white shirt with the top three buttons opened and the sleeves fastidiously rolled above the elbows; a blue bathing suit with a white stripe along each flank; and a pair of leather sandals. Animals had died for his footwear.

I fell into sadness.

Eliot said amicably, comparing me and Leah, "You really can tell you two are brother and sister. It's astonishing, actually."

"It's what happens," I said, "when you fuck each other year after year."

"Tramp!"

"It's true, Leah. People begin to look alike."

Eliot Howard touched his specs, jangling my reflection, and turned bashfully away. "My wife and I, I'm afraid, didn't look a thing alike. What I'm trying to say is that we stopped making love."

"Jesus," I shouted, "do we care?"

I stared at the Atlantic, the water crashing to shore, the sunlight glittering on the jetty's wet black rocks.

Eliot Howard said nervously, "Have I done something to offend you, Dennis?"

"Dennis!" I was disgusted.

Leah glared at me. "Eliot and I have been looking at houses."

"You *and* Eliot!"

"We've found a little place on Court Street."

I blinked at her, then at Eliot Howard. "Hasn't she told you the truth yet?"

He removed his shades. "I'm very sorry," he said softly, "but I'm afraid I don't understand what I've done to upset everyone." He appealed to Leah.

She was a basket case with penitence. "This is all my fault,

Eliot. Dennis is really Tramp's dog and Tramp's real name isn't Dennis but Aldo Huxley. He's my ex-boyfriend, not my brother, though he does have a real sister."

Eliot stared at her, then at me, struggling to achieve an intelligible version of things. Finally he stood up. "But I thought . . . you said . . ."

"She's a mental case, Eliot. Not to mention a bitch on wheels and an airhead. Without me she's nothing."

Leah told me to shut up. Then she shielded her eyes to see Eliot. "I'm awfully sorry, really. I like you extraordinarily. I can't honestly say why I haven't told you the truth. Please, forgive me."

Eliot Howard was, quite simply, devastated. "I've just been through a traumatic separation and a series of nervous breakdowns. I thought you two were my friends."

We watched the man turn and disappear down the beach. Leah laid back and covered her eyes with her arm.

"Nice play, Shakespeare!"

"Pipe down for once," she mumbled.

"I never figured you using some idle philistine nympholept to make me jealous. And incidentally, it didn't work."

She didn't move a muscle. A fly alighted on her gorgeous knee.

"Some rakish middle-aged breakdown case—"

"All you ever think about is yourself!"

"No one else does."

She rolled away. I addressed her back. "Some Republican divorcé with a penchant for asylums—"

"Kindly *shut up.* "

I counted to ten. "Mind if I ask where you've been the past several days?"

"Entertaining the football team, of course."

"With him!"

She sat up and threw sand with both hands. *"You're driving me crazy, Tramp! I'm losing my mind!"*

She started to cry. I opened my eyes and peered through my fingers. The sun was upon us. By way of apology, I wanted to steal some of its mercy and give it to Leah, wrapped in ribbon. I took her in my arms.

"Don't cry. I'm sorry."

She beset me with her furious gray eyes. "Dearest, I hate to put this so bluntly, but like your dog, Dennis, you lack proper training." She stood up. "I think that is what this summer is really about: *training.* "

"Dennis and I are untrainable."

"In the long run," she persisted, "years from now, you will thank me for it."

"Untrainable. "

"By Labor Day you will simply not recognize yourself when you catch hold of your reflection."

"Stop hanging around with Eliot Howard!"

"Part of the training."

"Don't do it, Leah."

"We have such a very long way to go in so short a span of time." She smiled dangerously. "I'm afraid this time I'm going to bring you to your senses, Tramp. I'm through playing."

Apprehension made me avert my eyes. The sea was aqua in color and rolling in, rolling in, rolling in.

Leah said, "In the end I'm hopeful that we will each laugh about this summer. Of course, that's assuming you survive."

She dived into the churning Atlantic near the jetty. I didn't wait around to see if my avenger surfaced.

VII

FROM MY ATTIC ASYLUM OVERLOOKING THE SEA, I WAS AS HIGH as the morning sun. The jockstrap was wet, but it was the sand therein that made me shudder upon its first contact with my vitals. My cutoffs, conversely, were dry, though stiff as flaxen cloth from the crystallization of sea salt. I grabbed my Bahne and followed Dennis into the morning.

The sand was so hot at eleven that I had to interrupt my frantic transit to the sea and step upon the surfboard. My father was reading a book, *More Joy* . . . If questioned, I was prepared to perjure myself: I've just come from an arduous morning of torching and scraping the Doric columns of your porch.

He said, without altering his rapt attention upon the page, "Junior, if I'm ever going to be a bedroom Lothario, I've got to lose weight. Lots of it."

I bent my head to scrutinize an illustration's particular geometry. From my angle it seemed a man and a woman upon a chandelier of orgasmic recreation. "Is it advisable, Father, that we broadcast our prurient interest when it lacks socially redeeming value?"

He raised his face and, fighting the sun, squinted through one eye. "I'm too old to be discreet, Junior." He flipped the page: A man dogging a woman. Her genitals seemed the width and breadth of the Queens Midtown Tunnel, his member the size of a sightseeing bus. Life with Leah Summit passed before my eyes. "Last night," my father said, "Splendid Hedgeson inspired Daddy to renew his subscription to the human race."

"A father's girl friend is none of his son's business. Furthermore, this is a family beach. I advise you to wrap that treatise in a brown paper bag."

My father impatiently closed the book. " 'My days are few,' " he recited, eyes closed. " 'Let me alone, awhile, that I may take comfort a little, before I go whence I shall not return, to the land of darkness and gloom.' "

"Please!"

"Let Daddy put it to you another way, Junior. I haven't had an itch in three years. I'm just so damn glad I got it back and that one Miss Hedgeson knows where to scratch it that I'm speechless with happiness."

I stepped from my board and lifted it above my head, casting my father in shadow. "Daddy, you've lost your moral compass."

"Splendid's husband," he replied, undaunted, "will be in Tucson for a week, selling toothpaste. He's a man with a dysfunctional kidney who's hooked to a dialysis machine twice a week. Between you and me, Junior, I'll be with the better half for the same period it took God to rush creation into opening day. All I ask is that you tell your mother I've gone golfing with Walker Mills and the Bridge brothers. You read me?"

It was very hot; I needed a swim with the sharks. I fled the land in search of sure footing.

RECUMBENT UPON THE BOARD, STARING STRAIGHT UP WHILE rising and falling with the assault of waves, I observed a cumulonimbus reminiscent of Leo Tolstoy drift past. Tolstoy hated his wife but, after leaving her, died in a railroad station. Never mind that he was into his eighties; it seemed the sort of tale my father should know about. At the moment of my resolution, however, the board went crashing into the jetty. I went under, head first, into a glop of sea slime. Surfacing as I did, all green and horrified, only the gulls, diving for a closer look, attended to my survival.

I resolved to worry about my own ass.

GRANDMA HAD SET THE TABLE IN THE DINING ROOM; THIS SIGnaled company. I counted five settings and stared out the window screen into the night's whisperings. I tried to guess who was coming but got lost in the droning of the katydids.

Someone crossed the lawn, talking to herself. Despite the darkness, I could tell by the meter of her steps that it was Grandma. A collar's jingling indicated that Dennis was following her. She made him sit before awarding him the treat. This resurrected memories of Grandpa feeding Dennis roast beef bones, albeit Grandpa himself was now a pile of bones.

"Now sit!" Grandma said. "I said sit! *Sit,* doggie!"

Thereafter, nothing but the crunching of bone. I flicked on the porch light: Dennis turned—chewing his bone with his ass in the air—and his eyes flashed green. Behind him Leah Summit stood in the arms of a man.

Naturally, when I charged down the steps, I ruined my own paint job.

"You remember Eliot Howard," Leah said.

I said to him, "It's something of a fucking horror show seeing your arms around my wife."

"She's not your wife. We've had a long talk about you."

"Don't you ever touch my wife again, you got that?"

"I know you know," Leah said softly, "that I'm not your wife."

"I'll cut it off, Howard. Off!"

Leah grabbed me by the shoulders and began shaking. "You listen to me, Tramp. I closed on my house this afternoon. Eliot's been living in a motel. I said he could have the back room, and he was just *thanking* me."

"What!"

"The back room!"

I glanced at Eliot and then at Leah. She still held my shoulders; I took one step forward and rested my forehead on her right one. "Why, Leah?"

"Training, sweetie."

Wisely, Eliot suggested that he leave. I lifted my head. When the breakdown case turned to open the door of his sports car, I said, "I could wipe you all over the street and blow my nose in your face. You better watch it!"

He slid into the seat and started the motor. "I'll show you that flooring tomorrow," he told Leah, and slipped on his mirror sunglasses.

When he drove away Leah kicked me square in the shinbone. "I know what you're up to, damn it, and I don't like it."

Looking up at her, I said, "Some wife I've got!" and put my arms up to protect myself from imminent slaps.

"I'm renting Eliot Howard a room in exchange for carpentry work. That's my final word."

I started to stand; Leah put her foot against my shoulder and kicked me over.

Grandma appeared at the front door. "I got baked apples that need coring, Leah!" She smiled until she noticed my face, the derangement thereon. "You just go wash your hands and face, Sonny, and change that tune of yours!"

Passing, Leah said forlornly, "In case you've forgotten, we were supposed to be married today."

THE DINNER CONSISTED OF BORSCH, BAKED TOMATOES TOPPED with parsley and bread crumbs, mashed potatoes with sautéed onions, string beans and almonds, marinated mushrooms, cottage cheese and chives, salad and barbecued chicken. Grandma and Mommy sat at the ends of the table, Teresa on one side and Leah Summit and I on the other. Grandma wore her company apron and a necklace of white pearls; our mother a gray housecoat and sunglasses.

"We got to wait a minute for the food because Teresie wants to say a prayer." Grandma turned to my sister. "Don't make it so long that the food gets cold. I don't think God wants us to let the food get cold on his account. Grandpa had a beautiful personality and God killed him like he was a fly."

Teresa bowed her head. "May we learn not to do unto others," she said simply, "what we would not have them do unto us. Amen."

Well, not a word about singing rock songs, taking drugs to enliven a weary spirit, reveling in the Laodicean and sybaritic; nothing about being the nation's valentine or resenting failure more than death everlasting; nothing about the scatology of human history, from which our collective heart has emerged wizened and worm-ridden.

All the same, Grandma stepped to the buffet table to make each of our plates a little universe of perfection. When each was served she returned to her seat and kept her eyes on her plate, as she always has, waiting for the reviews.

I said, with too much mashed potatoes in my mouth, "Grandma, your cooking keeps me from hammering nails into my heart."

My mother, disputably less rational than I, followed; she tapped her water glass with a spoon and stood. We all turned to her. For a moment she experienced a sudden paroxysm of tics, in which her face fluttered unprettily. "For some time now," she announced, "I have endured the most unspeakable unhappiness. Tomorrow, therefore, I am leaving for California. I cannot say when or if I shall return. In the meantime, if you'll each excuse me, I shall retire for the evening."

She passed through the living room, curtains sailing from the open windows in her wake.

There was no point in following her. I knew that she wouldn't be there, would in truth be lost in a depressive funk of insoluble grief. There comes a time when only prescription chemicals can help.

Grandma ventured to corral any misapprehensions. "Mommy ain't upset on account of Sonny and Leah ain't married today like they should be. No, she just don't enjoy life no more and ruins it for everybody else. It's a tragedy." She turned to Teresa. "Everything just happens so fast, honey. That's what's wrong with people. First Grandpa died on the steps and then your accident. Scotty was so nice. I seen so many people live and die, it's like I've been in a war my whole life."

We sat there respectfully as Grandma chewed her string beans.

"Daddy always bought Mommy firsthand appliances from the best shops in town," she said to Teresa. "He always got her the nicest colored help, too. After me, Mommy was the first to have an electric stove in town. She was a beautiful bride. They was both very attractive people. People thought they was famous, they was so attractive. We had the wedding ceremony at the Ocean Hotel that ain't there no more. We all got drunk and went for a swim. It wasn't so cold then. It was a beautiful ocean once. Then one day you wake up and know you should be dead. It's a shame."

Grandma turned and stared inconsolably at Leah and me. "I ain't never seen a pair of two people look so nice together."

Leah got up in a reflex of discomfort to clear the salad plates. Grandma watched her disappear into the kitchen before whispering angrily at me, "It's a shame Sonny's such a dope! Leah clears so beautifully!"

Sometime before coffee I fled to the porch and stepped into the night. Stars and silence: summertime, with all its natural shocks.

Leah came outside. I was sitting next to Dennis when she sat down beside me. "Poor Grandma," she said.

I laid my head on her lap. A breeze wafted above us, rattling the sycamore leaves. "Why did you buy that house?"

"Good investment, I guess."

"No other reason?"

"Well, there's my father dying of cancer, and I can't stand watching him."

I closed my eyes and made a duck noise. Then I did a cat. Then I began to moan.

Leah put her hands over both my temples and massaged them until I settled down. "Want to see the house?"

We walked along beneath the street lamps, Leah's ephemeral hand in mine, Dennis following behind with his bone, shaking his head back and forth, growling like a lunatic. Sure, a fragment of heaven fallen to earth. I, however, tend to ruin good things. "Promise me that you haven't slept with him."

We crossed the inlet, the water below us black and the moon's reflection shimmering in an aqueous path. We turned south.

"Eliot's been very kind to me, Tramp."

"Because I think I'd die if I heard you ever applied your avocado oil and performed miracles."

"Of course I haven't slept with Eliot!"

"But you realize he's hanging around until you do."

"Frankly, I'm sick of trying to figure out what men want from women." She grabbed my arm and stopped. "This is it."

I turned. The house was set behind two maple trees and a fence that was missing every other picket. The house was small, of Colonial influence, and leaned noticeably to the east. At one time, perhaps not many years after, say, the Civil War, the place had been painted white. To the side, down an oblong grass-covered driveway, stood a red carriage house; it too leaned to the east.

"Your own house." I stood there thinking: in your own house you can lock the door and hide; you can peek from behind the curtains into the world and make sure the window is locked.

"Come see the backyard." She took my hand and we walked up the driveway, passing two sets of bay windows. The yard was enclosed by cedar trees and seemed to extend forever into the darkness.

"The soil's not very good," Leah said sensibly. "Mostly sand after four inches, but I'll bring in horse manure and have a marvelous garden." She looked at me. "It will be the most beautiful little house you've ever seen. If I want to, I can sell it and make a nice profit. Eliot's room is behind that window." She nodded to the rear of the house.

"You listen to me, Leah. Men like Eliot Howard sneak into your bed after you're asleep and slam it in without you ever knowing."

Leah has a habit of ignoring my frequent admonitions. "The house needs completely new plumbing and electric systems. Eliot's going to do the plumbing and I'm learning about electricity. I've got stacks and stacks of books on foundations, sewer lines, furnaces, insulation, taxes."

"Electricity is dangerous, and all this Eliot Howard wants to do is put his plumbing into your socket."

"All one needs," Leah said calmly, "is a little electricity tester and it's perfectly safe."

I was not happy. "How much?"

"Twenty-one."

"Do you get it back if it falls over?"

"Drop dead!"

Leah lifted the backyard's gate from its latch and began swinging it back and forth. After the fifth swing it dropped off its hinge and fell on her toe.

"I know you're using this Howard to torture me. I can assure you that it's working to perfection."

"I'm not using anyone. He's helping me and I'm helping him. He's had a very difficult couple of years."

My hands were covering my ears. "I can't hear you, Summit."

"When he was institutionalized in Massachusetts, he learned carpentry. The poor man has lived in a motel for two months."

I dropped my hands. "Were you talking to me?"

Leah walked off down the driveway.

I found her on the front porch. "Leah?"

She put her hands to her ears. I stared at the stars, at the street lamps, which ran in a long row all the way to the Atlantic. We sat on the porch a long time in silence. Finally Leah let me hold her hand.

"Did I tell you I quit my job at the Kafe?"

"Oh?"

"The bartender pressed up against me in a state of arousal. I had to scream to get him away."

I smiled; virtue rewards itself.

Leah said, "Shall we go back to Grandma's for coffee now?"

"Allow me first to kill the bartender and Eliot with one punch."

Leah stood and began to walk away.

"Wait!"

She began to run. "I will," she called, "until Labor Day."

I ran after her, but lost her while crossing the Shark River Bridge.

She wasn't with Grandma nor with her family. Clearly the problem between Leah Summit and me was Eliot Howard.

THE FOLLOWING MORNING GRANDMA STOOD ON THE FRONT porch, transfixed by something in Teresa's garden. She pointed to a columbine. "Ain't it beautiful!" I spotted a hummingbird dart into the shadows and hover momentarily in a trapezoid of sunlight. I put my coffee cup on the porch railing and sat on a little wicker stool.

"What's Teresa think she's doing?" I pointed to my sister, sitting in her wheelchair by the birdbath.

"Your sister prays for the world an hour every morning." Grandma shook her head. "Someone who used to be so happy, Sonny. Like you."

"I never have been happy, Grandma."

She waved her hand dismissingly, sat in her wicker rocker and picked up her book. When the sulfur match flared, she glanced from the book to observe me lighting a cigarette. "Uncle Jack got his voice box cut out from smoking. After that it killed him in his sleep."

"If it isn't one thing," I said, "then it's nine others."

Grandma watched a gang of children ride past on their bicycles. "I hate to think about dying, Sonny. Whenever I do, I have to put on the TV."

She patted her hair and returned to her book. Then she looked up. "Oh yes, Sonny. Junkyard Mills called this morning asking for Daddy. Ain't that a dumb joke, after you said they was together at the golf field? And then Daddy called you. I got a number inside you got to call back right away. Daddy said it was important."

"Where's Mommy?"

"Up in her room with the door locked tight, waiting for the cab taking her to the airport. She's going to her sister's for a while. I ain't never cried so much in my life."

Grandma smoothed the ruffles of her dress, pink with little blue flowers. "I got to go inside and get started. The House of Retarded Christians is coming over with Teresa for a luncheon party, and I got to cook for thirty."

Grandma stared into the morning, into the leaves rattling in the hot ocean breeze, before turning in desperation. "Ain't there something you can do, Sonny?"

I lowered my eyes and spoke softly. "I'd better call our provider."

I phoned from the pantry. Peeking through the curtains, I studied Teresa praying for the world while birds splashed in Grandpa's antique birdbath. Prayer: Talking at someone on the phone after they've dropped the receiver into the toilet.

An Englishwoman answered. "Splendid Hedgeson speaking."

I asked for Mr. Bottoms.

"I'm afraid you've rung up the wrong line, dearie."

"There's not a big fat man there?"

"Why, you must mean Mr. Haliburton. Hold the line while I fetch him."

Then, "Richard Haliburton speaking."

"Daddy?"

"Ah, Mr. Huxley!"

"What?"

"Yes, yes. I know very well that my *Book of Marvels* is out of print. Now, about those reprint rights!"

I took the receiver from my ear and stared at it. Then I heard my father's voice change to its normal inflection.

"All right, Junior, Splendid's gone now. Little game of mine created to protect the innocent. Now listen carefully."

"You've got your nerve, calling here! And why didn't you tell Walker Mills to play along?"

"No talking in the ranks, mate. Daddy's calling because he forgot about a little matter, which he's ordering his boy to take care of."

"People like you," I shouted, "accelerate the demise of empires."

"Now hear this, Junior: Some buyers are scheduled to inspect the Resort today. Condominium people who want to demolish and rebuild. I could make a fortune, so you be on the porch like you're running things or else be prepared to face court-martial and eviction."

I announced this was the last favor I would ever execute for him, notwithstanding an appearance at his funeral, and asked when to expect them.

"That's one more question about life I can't answer. You call the real estate people and ask. And one more thing! Perhaps you can tell me what the man with the twenty-inch penis ate for breakfast this morning."

"*What?*"

"I say, the man with the twenty-inch penis!"

"I'm hanging up, Father."

"Well, Junior, I had myself two eggs from Splendid's fridge and two sli—"

MY MOTHER STRUGGLED DOWN THE VARNISHED STAIRWAY WITH two suitcases dragging alongside. Her hair was tightly bunned and her eyes expressed all the unhappiness of fifty years of seconds that had escorted her to this disastrous urgency for self-exile. She was wrapped in a heavy wool sweater and skirt.

"Mom, it was eighty-five degrees this morning."

She stopped at the base of the steps. "Good morning, dear. I don't care if your father sleeps with other women. I suppose I once minded, but I don't any longer. There's really no use denying it another moment. And anyway, the weatherman said it was in the thirties."

"Celsius, Mother. This is July. *July!*"

My mother looked askance. "I'm afraid a woman could simply freeze to death in July with that man, dear," and she began sliding her bags toward the front door.

"Jesus Christ, Mother, *I'll* do that."

She smiled, lost in a trance of prescribed disorientation. "I know how much you hate to do things for others, dear. I didn't want to have to ask you."

She went directly outside and I carried her bags to the porch. She put her arms around herself. We watched Grandma wheeling Teresa up the ramp at the side of the house. My mother called good-bye to them, went down the front steps and turned grandly to the house, as if for the last time.

"Ever since I can remember I have felt all alone here." She closed her eyes and put her face to the sun. Her sorrow was as evident as her craziness, and for a moment the two seemed as complementary as life and death.

A yellow cab pulled to the curb. I followed my mother to the street, carrying her bags. Grandma and Teresa watched from the porch. My mother called, "Go inside, it's too cold for everyone today!" and stepped into the cab. The driver and I arranged her luggage in the trunk, then I stood in the gutter and looked at her through the open window.

"Good-bye, Mom."

"Terminal," she told the driver, and looked at herself in a hand mirror.

The cab made a U turn at the beach and came back up the street. My mother blew me a kiss. "God blesss you, dear," she cried. Then she was gone, down the street, beneath the trees' arching darkness.

Breakdowns

I

TOWARD THE END OF JULY, FOR WHAT SEEMED AN INTERMINA-
ble seven days of rain, I lugged my guitar back and forth from
Manhattan. As part of my new manager's design for my official
August premiere, I played the Park Avenue Cafe, Lewis Friedman's Snafu, the Botany Talk House and Eric's. With the
exception of Eric's—a genteel bar and eatery for the conven-
tionally vacuous, with a special back room for the musically
anonymous—the places were singularly squalid dives, each
equidistant from Union Square, a little park where unemploya-
bles push dope and kill each other. I rode the number 7 bus
to the square from Penn Station, carrying my guitar and amp
through the rainy twilight of urban derangement, the specter
of assault hastening my step.

Still, no one killed me; rather, I died by my own hand
onstage.

At the Park Avenue Cafe, for example, three people drank
at the bar, their backs to me, shouting at one another while I
played to five empty tables from a tiny platform in a corner
near the men's room. Beyond the tables, above the backs of the

three customers, through the window, I could see a section of a bank sign flashing LOW INTEREST in red neon.

I played for half an hour, seven songs, and no one once clapped. Afterward the bartender brought me a drink on the house: payment.

The Botany Talk House and Snafu gigs were just as unspeakable, just as unseemly. These places, however, advertise in the rear of the *Village Voice*. My name appeared on pages 74 and 75 in the last issue of July. Under "Botany Talk House" in a one-inch black-print square:

TRAMP

BOTTOMS

WEDNESDAY

JULY 30

Under the Snafu logo and address, my name was listed along with such aspirant big shots as Rozinski Avedon, Concepto and the Nervous Systems, Bloody Mary and the Hygenists, and the Commotions. I didn't mention the advertisements to anyone but Dennis; he seemed impressed, chasing his tail. At the Talk House, I played beneath alternating red-and-blue spotlights in a small room that was painted crimson. The audio system only periodically distorted, and during the second set only half the tables were empty, half the number that were empty for the first one.

Snafu, meanwhile, featured a bowling game at the entrance, which several of the more rarefied customers found more engrossing than my performance. Alternatively, the second set overflowed with impatient Rozinski Avedon loyalists who just couldn't find the time between beers and pills to applaud the heresy of my non–New Wave ways. In the end my share of the door amounted to the price of the round-trip train ride, plus a cheese sandwich and coffee at a Penn Station greasy spoon.

During the Eric's gig, a thunderstorm hit the city. Lightning crackled in the speakers, mangling the circuitry, and the radio call voice of a Latin American cabbie accompanied me through "Fear and Trembling," which terminated prematurely when the lighting imploded and the speakers died with a high-voltage pop.

The manager apologized for the blackout and suggested we arrange a new date. I said my people would be in touch; this was a joke, a bit of inaccessible drollery, and I chaperoned my amp and guitar cases into the rain, misunderstood and mistreated.

I was soaked, and sitting in an air-conditioned train for two hours was exactly what anyone's mother would advise if her progeny wanted a cold. When I got home Dennis was waiting on the porch, mashing a stick. I bent down to kiss him and sneezed right in his face.

THE FIRST DAYS OF AUGUST PASSED AS SLOWLY AS A HEAD COLD. Further, no one seemed to be where they once were, or where I expected them to be. All I could find were notes throughout the house, written at different times and back and forth to different people. For instance:

Sonny,
    Grandma's gone to the fruit and vegetable stand with Mrs. Fischgrund. Dennis messed in the living room and it took me all morning to clean up. That ain't the Sonny Grandma remembers!

Junior,
    Have gone with Splendid Hedgeson to a retreat in the Catskills. I'm counting on you to keep the ship on course. Be loyal to your name.
Sincerely,
Your Commander-in-Chief

Most Fanciful One,

I'm off to Manhattan for a few more days of work with my editor. The second part of my book is giving me fits.

Ardently,
The Girl of Your Dreams

I lounged in bed in my pajamas, consumed bowl after bowl of Grandma's vegetable soup and wrote "Sickness."

Upon recovery I ran in the mornings to avoid Eliot Howard and set to work afternoons with a scraper and ethylene torch to remove the blisters of four-year-old paint from the front porch's Doric columns.

The rain persisted. I kept dry beneath a Marine Corps poncho with bullet holes, taped closed, in the hood.

On one such rainy morning the phone rang. I answered: "Leah!"

"My guy?"

"Mary Wells?"

I informed Owen that I'd tried to reach him for more than a week.

"Alas," he said, "guy's manager has only recently returned from Bimini with a pretty boy who deals big stuff," and sniffed in such a way that I inferred the substance to be something other than snot. I conceded that my four gigs hadn't sounded much better and announced my retirement from the pop 'n' roll circuit.

"Now you listen to me, guy. Rock is our redemption, our wafer and wine. It shall never die, because we make it live. Rock is God, guy. Do you follow?" He sniffed again. "Guy?"

"I'm here, Owen."

"I'd like to get down to business with you. May I?"

I granted permission and listened to Owen improvise on a piano in the background.

"Three things," he said. *"Numero uno,* I need a live version of my gigolo's musical canon. There's simply no other way we can construct a show of gaga proportions. *Numero* two, your manager brunched yesterday with a boy from JP's and hit him with guy's End demo, which guy's manager produced stealthily on his mixing board. The JP boy was monstrously impressed. He's offered the door, plus one ad in the *Voice* and *Soho.* This shall be our premiere, guy. It is now inevitable. It is going to happen one week from tonight, at nine P.M. Is my minstrel gigolo still there?"

"Here, Owen."

"Lastly, guy, Torrey has been rubbing her noodle over your failure to call."

"I'm confused, Owen. Deeply so."

"So is she, guy. Super confused. But what has my pimpsterdom got to do with when guy and his manager are going to connect for a performance? Personally, I feel you should agree that tomorrow is a right-on idea."

I told Owen I didn't need to check my calendar.

"Fine. Now three more things. *Uno,* meet your manager at his loft at one PM for a session on a newly tuned Hardman upright. Two, be prepared to discuss basic production ideas for a tape of guy's five best songs—studio time and musicians donated by guy's heavenly-trim, narrow-hipped super manager. Thirdly, the king of rock, alias my guy, must begin to think practically about what artists must do in order *to happen* in this world of capitalist reality. Is guy tuned into Owen's oracle?"

"Committing this to memory, Owen."

"Then are we prepared to go for it with tasteless singlemindedness?"

"There are," I offered, "the Jagger-ravaged minds of children to think about restoring."

"Truly, guy. The children indeed. We must make them love you. Must make them dish out mega allowances for guy and his manager. Because there is a world of difference between our ideal and the world's real. Are you with me, guy?"

"Tomorrow, yes."

He said *"Abrazos"* and the phone went dead.

I returned to the porch. Merrill Miller's gang had congregated before the front steps to taunt Dennis, who was rubbing his eyes clownishly.

I am not stupid. I have a secret knowledge, about which I am reticent. Nonetheless, consider this: Why should God award medals when humanity hasn't yet developed a chest to pin them on? Merrill Miller didn't know; none of them did. "Sermon on the Porch," I announced and, gazing at my little friends, declaimed this gnosis: "My children, if you bring forth what is within you, what you bring forth will save you. But if you do not bring forth what is within you, what you do not bring forth will destroy you."

Merrill Miller screamed, "You're stupid as a dead moth! I'll get my knife and cut you in half!"

He and his gang ran off in the rain, slapping their asses and making Indian noises.

"Ye of little faith!" I called after.

THE DAY HAD TURNED TO NIGHT FROM THE RAIN. THE BEACH House School van stopped before the house with its headlights dancing luminously in the rain. Carver, the one-armed black man, wheeled Teresa down a ramp and then up the front walk. Teresa held a black umbrella above them. I went down to help.

Two children, two boys, trailed obediently behind her, their heads as round as balloons. At one time they were known as Mongolian Idiots. Now, I'm afraid, they are called Special

People. Carver shook my hand with his left—as his right was a hook. Thereafter, my sister and the children and I went inside.

They were wet. I suggested a fire and commenced collecting logs from the basement. Teresa went to the kitchen to make a pot of tea.

When the flames leaped from the paper, we were situated around the fireplace. The room flickered with shadows and the children stared in astonishment. I made a face at the sadder one; he covered his mouth with both hands and his narrow eyes wrinkled in the corners. I did the same to the other; his mouth opened when he laughed and sent drool down his chin.

A car door slammed and I stepped to the screen door. Eliot Howard, smartly attired in a fisherman's blue raincoat, trotted up the path through the puddles. He came inside and shook dry. Then I introduced him. After all the lies he'd accepted, it was impossible to know whether or not he believed that Teresa was my sister.

"Jesus, Eliot," I said, "quit looking so damn solemn."

"I've just come from Leah's new house," he said portentously. "We were laying the new floor when the police came." He lowered his eyes.

"Police?"

He cleared his throat and put his hand on my shoulder. "It's Leah's father, Tramp. He's dead."

I blinked at him.

"His neighbor found him in the car this afternoon. I thought you might want to be with Leah. She's devastated."

I couldn't breathe. "A crash?"

"The car never left the garage. The police said he hooked a vacuum cleaner hose to the exhaust pipe and ran it through the front window."

I stared out the door: rain striking the road. When I turned back, Eliot was smiling tragically at my sister. I looked all over the house for my poncho before I realized I was wearing it. Then I ran.

I STOOD ON THE MILK BOX AND PEERED IN HER KITCHEN WIN-
dow. She was holding a teakettle in her right hand and staring into the blue flames curling off the burner. I thought, *one day Leah Summit will die,* and started to faint. Lightning flashed in a long scimitar, made me jump, and Leah turned to the window.

I foundered to the kitchen door. The down spout was clogged and water cataracted steadily over the gutters onto my hood. Leah stepped outside in her own poncho and opened an oversized red umbrella.

"Walk with me."

We turned east at the street, toward the Atlantic. I gazed at her for quite some time; she was staring straight ahead.

"I'm sorry, Leah. I didn't like him, but I'm sorry."

"Oh, let's not talk."

We held hands in silence all the way to the beach. The Atlantic churned gray and wild, and the waves crashed onto the sand as loud as wailing. The wind ravaged Leah's umbrella, which tumbled away from us like a crippled red bird. Then we both stood very still in green ponchos, watching clouds racing inland, low and the color of slate.

Leah put her arm around my waist. When I turned to her, she was still facing the water. "I never really knew him," she said flatly. "Now I never will."

Her hood filled with wind and blew backward like a behead-
ing. I bowed mine to keep from losing it.

"All those years I never saw him, never came home. The way I ignored him. Thinking I was so much brighter, that my life was somehow too important to be burdened."

She turned to me, her black hair soaked and glistening and her face coppery from a month of summer; but her gray eyes, gray as the Atlantic, were as sorrowful as I'd ever seen them.

"Why do we always learn too late, Tramp?"

"Not always," I whispered.

"Too late for me and him."

"Not for us, maybe."

Leah turned back to the Atlantic. "I didn't even know he was sick until seven weeks ago. He's been sick for two years and I didn't even know it."

I told her I didn't think the dead ever wanted to live as bad memories, and she put her face into my chest. I touched her hair.

"I feel deserted, Tramp."

I put my arms around her and watched the waves, felt her heart beating through the ponchos. "Don't cry."

After a while she leaned away and stared at me. I can't say whether it was rain or tears that pearled in her eyelashes. "When we die," she said, "do you think we could do it together?"

"I think so."

"How about in life?"

I closed my eyes. "I hope so."

The rain was cold and Leah was all against me.

"Do you know what I loved about you, Tramp?"

"I swear to God I don't."

"You had a way of keeping loneliness away from me. Now I'm lonely all the time."

I looked up into the rain, into the moving clouds, and Leah rested her head against my shoulder.

When she handed me the piece of yellow paper, I unfolded it and the ink streaked in the rain.

Everything's been cared for. The machines are tuned like new. I hurt like hell. War's over.

IT SEEMED TO RAIN FOREVER AND EVER. I RETURNED WITH Leah to her mother's house and administered to orders from the kitchen. When I first encountered Mrs. Summit, she was sitting in the living room amid family and friends. They all knew me, of course, and their antipathy wasn't at all redolent of a bathroom air freshener. Mrs. Summit's hair was grotesquely fluffed, and she wore a pair of gray-framed sunglasses the size of binoculars.

I handed her a cup of coffee with saccharine fizzing ominously from the bottom. "Mrs. Summit, I'm very sorry."

She took my hand. "Hon," she said, "the world's just lost a whole lot of a classy man today," and quickly turned away.

At midnight the rain stopped. I tucked Leah into bed in her old bedroom, where we first made love, and watched her swallow the sleeping pills. I held her hand until I heard her fall asleep. Then I went downstairs, found Mrs. Summit asleep in the living room and went outside. I stuck my head into the garage. The car just sat there. I thought about where Mr. Summit might be, but not for very long.

That night the stars appeared for the first time in a week. I walked south to Avon-by-the-Sea. I stopped in front of Leah's new house, where Eliot Howard was laying the floor by lamplight. I thought, the world is overpopulated with loneliness, and walked through puddles wherein moons shined. Then I went straight to the attic and, sitting at the electric piano, composed "Driven to Death."

AT DAWN THE SMELL OF GREENERY CATAPULTED INTO THE AIR, and the sky, clear and limitless, reflected in puddles underfoot. Dennis walked beside me, step for step, on our way to the beach, which was soaked to the color of khaki. The ocean, green at the horizon and blue toward shore, unfurled toward us quietly as Mahler's Fourth. The sea gulls, naturally, were scavenging for storm victims, and Dennis, just as naturally, dashed seaward to frighten them. With a similar instinct I hummed "Driven to Death" on my way to the Seaside Cafe, famous for its selection of pop/rock historical smashes—assuming you were of particularly melancholic extraction.

Dennis sat outside the window staring at my wheat toast. I drank my coffee, flavored with cream and honey, to Tom Rush's immortal cover of Ms. Mitchell's "Circle Game." I marveled at the lyrics' trenchancy as Dennis began to drool imploringly. I ordered his favorite, oatmeal toast and cream cheese, and laid it on a napkin on the sidewalk. This gave umbrage to the chintzy types at the counter who skimp and order white toast with margarine for themselves. Of course, Dennis does not appreciate the wonder of my empathy; he expects it as payment for enduring me as his master.

Well, Neil Young's "Round and Round," Dylan's "Positively 4th Street," Robert Palmer's instant classic "Johnny and Mary," which provoked more looks from the counter reactionaries, and finally, Rundgren's incomparable evocation of rending loss, "Last Ride." I ordered more coffee, smoked two cigarettes and watched the summer sun arch higher and higher above the Atlantic. I paid up when Jimmy Webb's version of Boudleaux Bryant's "Love Hurts" clicked off.

Going outside, I thought, five years from now, someone like me—someone with nothing but his dog and a brain intractable with illusions—will sit down in a café somewhere and play "Driven to Death" and decide that life, given death, doesn't need justification.

When I stepped into the full glare of morning an Avanti passed on Ocean Drive carrying two fat passengers. I thought: No, the man wouldn't dare! Meanwhile, Dennis jumped into the air and bit my waving hand. This provoked a little scene on the corner, a contest of sorts in which I attempted to remove Dennis' collar before he could grab my wrist. Dennis, however, deficient in irony, lost perspective, got riled and ripped the arm of my sweat shirt cleanly from its socket stitching. Then he wanted my pants. I was up against the wall, begging and pleading, when a genteel elderly couple hobbled past. Dennis, you understand, was simply *preparing* to attack, hunching before me with a scheming intelligence in his eyes; this much the couple could not see. Furthermore, I have long hair, and the aged, who tend to be benighted to begin with, possess the patience and prejudice of fascists. They glowered at my ostensible display of paranoid oddness. I waved and shouted. This hurried them around the corner. Dennis watched them go out of sight, then lunged.

GRANDMA AND SADIE FISCHGRUND WERE ROCKING ON THE porch sipping tea and gossiping about Mr. Summit's suicide.

"Sonny, you remember my friend Mrs. Fischgrund."

I was joyous over "Driven to Death" and, shaking the woman's hand, said, "Mrs. Fischgrund, I presume!"

She turned to Grandma, as she always has whenever she wishes to address me. "He was always scared of bees, Flora. I remember that like it was yesterday. He used to stand by my fire thorn and cry for his sister. She took care of him like a mother."

Well, this reminiscence, calcified into uselessness by two decades of disappointments, marshaled us straight toward regret. I observed the house next door; the fire thorn still stood, and stood still.

Grandma asked what happened to "them nice pants I ironed" and I looked down at the several tears. "Dennis."

The terrier's ears stood up and he cocked his head. Grandma glared and waved an admonishing finger. "Bad dog! Doggie ain't supposed to tear pants. No!"

Sadie Fischgrund frowned. "Flora, do I smell our prunes?"

Grandma uttered a falsetto cry and struggled from the chair. "I forgot all about them damn prunes, Sadie!"

I trailed Grandma into the kitchen, disinclined to hear Mrs. Fischgrund's tales of her *successful* grandchildren.

The phone rang and I had it before the second ring. "Leah!"

"Might someone help me into the tub?" Teresa asked.

When I reached her bedroom, behind the kitchen, I knocked twice, heard "Okay" and entered.

The room was bright with columns of sunshine that illuminated dust spiraling above her bed and bureau. On the top of the bureau, low enough that a person seated, say, in a wheelchair could reach her socks in the top drawer, rested my sister's collection of Raggedy Anns.

This was Saturday and my twin was languishing in bed with reading glasses, a ponytail, a red cotton nightgown. My sister is proof of God, I thought, and of God's contemptible faults, and sat on the bed beside her.

"Been reading a book of yours," she said.

"*Heart of Darkness?*"

In fact, she was reading *The Political Economy of Human Rights*. This one wasn't mine; the one that was, *The Nineteen Sixty-One Championship Yankees*, lay open at her side. She handed it to me, pointing.

I took the book and beheld my dream inscribed at age six: "I want too B moor famus then Micky Mantel." Below that a picture of Mickey Mantle, excepting his face, over which I had glued a shot of my own face as it had appeared in the kindergarten class picture: crew cut, incipient madness flickering in my eyes.

Opening her arms to me, Teresa said, "Help me into the chair, Mickey."

She was small, the room smelled of lilacs, and I placed her in the wheelchair without shedding a tear.

"If you don't mind me saying so," she said solemnly, "you've not been very kind to Leah this summer. I hope you plan on changing."

The phone rang, I lunged. "Leah! Jesus, I could kill myself!"

"Junior?"

"*You!*"

"Brush your mop a time or two, and tango over here. I got a lady I want you to meet."

"Where are you?"

"Poolside."

"I don't think so."

"What's this we hear about Wharton Summit going into the dark?"

"He's dead."

"How the hell can he be dead when I saw him just last week punching that Proscuto slob so hard that his toupee fell off. Proscuto's, I mean."

"This happens," I said, "when we smoke the exhaust pipes of running engines. Not exactly your casual high."

I heard ice tinkle and then a swallow. "Well, Junior, some daddies cut it and others don't. You can't say the same for yours."

I watched Teresa wheel herself toward the bathroom.

"I will, however, say this much, Father. Your behavior has evolved from the execrable to the irremeable. *Look it up.* Salud."

Teresa was drawing her bath. Her narrow back was to me, and she had to speak above the splash of water. "Remember the little mask you wore when we took baths together?"

"I remember."

She turned to me, laughing, then threw a handful of oil beads into the tub. The water went blue, and I kneeled by her side to accelerate the dissolve with my hand.

"You were such an odd little boy, Mr. Bottoms. Your only friends were Leah and me, and you spent most of your time talking to the piano."

"Conversely," I said, "you were the normal one, dropping your dolls out the attic window to make their eyes fall out."

Teresa let down her hair. I can't think of many things better to do than making your sister smile. Then again, nostalgia is a prelude to depression. I went to the bedroom window and stared into the yard. A robin was murdering a worm; I gaped, horrified.

"I remember once," Teresa said, "I saw you walk past that window carrying a frozen dog over your shoulder."

I closed my eyes and pictured Jocko, my first dog, whom I'd found, after two days of searching, in a neighbor's bushes. A run-over case, the vet had confirmed.

Teresa shut off the bathwater. "Do you think Eliot Howard is handsome?"

I turned. "I think so. I also think he likes you."

"No!" She was mortified. "No, he doesn't." She averted her eyes shamefully. "No, really."

"I'll call him right now and ask."

"Don't you dare!"

When I smiled she told me to use the door. "I'm going to bathe now, tease."

"You want me to call Grandma?"

"I can manage by myself."

"None of us can manage by ourself, Teresa."

Pushing the bathroom door closed with her right hand, she blew me a kiss with her left.

I stood gawking at myself in the door's full-length mirror. Reflexively, I made all sorts of faces at that long-haired apparition which, one day, would be either a box of bones or a court jester in Satan's inferno circus. For example, I stuck out my tongue and then employed my pinkies to expand my nostrils, my thumbs to stretch my mouth and my middle fingers to pull down the flesh around my eyes. A credible ghoul. Just then Teresa opened the door.

"I need— *Oh my God!*"

"Wha'?" My thumbs were still in my mouth and I had commenced to drool.

"Stop that!"

"Why?"

"I need a washcloth."

"Ah geh ih!"

"Actually, it's an improvement."

When I came back with the cloth, I said "Eliot Howard" and made the face again.

She said "Jealous!" and slammed the door.

"I love Leah Summit," I shouted. "Why shouldn't I be jealous?"

I listened to Teresa lower herself into the tub.

"Why not tell Leah that?"

I looked up from my toes and stared my reflection straight in the eyes. It didn't have the answer, either.

NO ONE ANSWERED AT THE SUMMITS' HOUSE. THEY'D DOUBTLESS gone to the funeral home to dress Mr. Summit, now flooded with embalming fluid, for his stay in eternity. I turned around and headed for the Last Resort.

I walked into the lobby and confronted a sign above the register: CLOSED FOR RENOVATION. LEAVE. The dusty windows, opaque with sunlight, vibrated with the ocean breeze. I continued down the darkened hallway, passing empty rooms, and opened the screen door to the back patio. In the open sky a single-engine plane dragged a sign: SUICIDE PREVENTION HOTLINE 555-9188. I followed its transit until I spotted my father at treetop level. He was standing naked on the high diving board, a white bathing cap covering his hair and black-rimmed goggles protecting his eyes. His resemblance to an early aviator was in evidence, albeit he could hardly fly. The sound of his stomach smacking the water evoked a wince from both me and the naked woman splayed on a pool chaise. I, however, did not applaud.

My father noticed me on his way to a towel. "Pull up a drink and have a chair."

"Too early for a chair," I said.

"Standing then!"

The woman—Splendid Hedgeson, I presumed—said, "Actually, I rather can't *stand* drinking so early myself. I positively must have a seat in which to enjoy my liquor." She stretched for her cigarettes and spilled the drink. My father mopped up the mess and lit the woman's butt.

"Junior," he said, "my dear friend Heddy Spledgeson."

I nodded and looked away.

"It's Hedgeson, actually. Splendid Margaret Hedgeson." She blew smoke into the air and pointed to a cooler at the foot of the chaise. "There's heaps of goodies inside, dearie. Why not have a nice cream soda and a biscuit?"

Well, they were both drunk. I observed them. Death, after all, takes a long time, and we go through more rehearsals than we care to acknowledge. Meanwhile, out in the world, my father didn't know what to make of the wet towel he was holding; finally he simply tossed it into an empty chair.

"Junior," he said, "make double time upstairs and find Mrs. Hedgeson and Commander Bottoms two dry Resort towels."

I went indoors, removed the phone from the hook at the

decrepit registration desk and scooted to the second floor. I leaned out the window of room 2B. Mrs. Hedgeson was applying lotion to my father's shoulders.

"Daddy?"

Crowned by the bathing cap and goggles, he squinted at the building. "Reading you loud and clear, Junior."

"Come in here a minute, will you?"

"Splendid's in the middle of a dirty joke."

"Someone's on the phone for you."

"Business?"

"Realty people, I believe."

When he stood I dropped the towels out the window. Mrs. Hedgeson caught them.

"Do you fancy fish pies?" she called up. "I make extraordinary fish pies."

"I don't eat anything with eyes," I said, and ducked inside.

I got on the phone in the upstairs landing and listened to my father walking down the hallway. When he picked up the receiver, I said, "I'm calling from the Face Reality Company to suggest you've forgotten or ignored the basic rules of life in the twentieth century."

"That you, Walker?"

"*No!* It's your goddamn son calling to ask about what the hell's going on!"

"Now *you* read *me*, Junior. I know reality better than ever. I'm a bankruptcy case with a wife gone AWOL and a moocher for a son who broke his family's heart by betraying a young woman and betraying his talent for serious music; and then, still not satisfied, broke up the family, having nothing better to do. There's a commandment against dishonoring a boy's mom and dad, and I suggest you stand accused."

"Bullshit."

"The fact is you came home with your myriad and sundry

mental problems, no job, a canceled wedding, no place to live, and within the month the cottage's burnt toast, my wife's gone, I'm forced to leave my own home for peace and quiet, and my best friend asphyxiates himself in grievance for his daughter. Then the Resort goes under. That's the *reality* of the situation!"

"The reality," I shouted, "is that you're drunk at eleven A.M.—"

"It's five o'clock in Tokyo, buster!"

"Shame," I whispered. "Shame on you."

"What?"

"Shame . . . on . . . you."

"Those who live in glass houses—"

I drop-kicked the phone and hurried downstairs. My father was leaning on the registration desk, his back to me, still barking into the phone: ". . . between consulting adults who are lonely . . ."

I ran outside, into the light.

I STUCK A NOTE ON THE FRONT DOOR HANDLE OF LEAH'S NEW home:

> I can't ever find you. I'm going to NYC to see my new manager. No one ever asks about my career. A musician's only appreciated after he's dead.
>
> Tramp

The train's windows were tinted green; the industrial landscape slid greenly past. With train rides there is a beginning and an end. In between, hearing the tick of the tracks, you think about such things as lifetimes: Wharton Summit, Leah and I, my mother and father, Leah and I, Teresa as we knew her, Dennis, Leah and I, Grandma and the insurance-table odds against her going another year, Leah and I, Leah and I, Leah and I. Perhaps it was the tint of the windows that made me think of water. Specifically of Leah taking a bath; of how I would sit on the front porch of that crooked white house beneath the rosebush. The front door would be open, it would be springtime and I would hear movement in the bathwater.

Two hours later the inevitable terminal, subterranean and smelling of steam and iron. Then the ascension of stairs in artificial light toward more artificial light; crowds, announcements of trains and, from below, the shrieking of metal brakes on metal tracks. Finally, the street: columns of miasmal sunlight between skyscrapers; the heat and exhaust of interminable traffic; the dangerous promise of redemption always one block away, always around the next corner.

Owen Chance's loft was three stories above an Italian restaurant on Spring Street. I buzzed, said "Tramp" into the intercom and climbed the dark flight of stairs. Owen, palpably hung over, was standing in the doorway, shirtless, in black pajama pants, blue suede shoes and a pair of round black-lensed sunglasses.

"Born to die, guy," he said hoarsely. "Born to go to hell. Tattooed on my you know what. Come in."

The loft, gymnasium size, was all darkness and stale air.

"Your presence," Owen said, facing away, "forces me to presume it is daytime."

"Afternoon in fact."

He limped toward the kitchen, his hands pressing his ears, and started a pot of coffee. Then he rummaged through a leather bag, located a vial and tossed two pills down the hatch.

"Black Beauties," he explained.

I inferred *speed* and walked toward an overhead spotlight that illuminated Owen's Hardman upright. Sunlight splintered through the black curtains, and I felt the claustrophobic craving to fling them open. Beside me a raised platform, large enough for a band, was cluttered with ashtrays, a telephone, a box of tissues, empty beer cans and cigarette packs, a *Rolling Stone*, a bottle of aspirin, headphones, sheet music. Next to the platform stood a mixing board, an amplifier surmounting a chair, a microphone stand on its side, drums disassembled beneath the piano, a xylophone keyboard without legs canted against the wall, a synthesizer flashing red lights.

Owen came from the stove and weltered in the mess, searching for a cigarette. I thought, I could make a run for it, our agreement is only verbal; I could deny ever meeting him. Instead I stopped at the stove and lowered the flame beneath the coffee. When I turned to ask Owen if he took milk and sugar, he was standing behind me smoking a cigarette. His mascara had smeared badly, and the radiating smell of perfume was redolent of an all-night lust carnival.

"The difference between him and me," Owen said, "is he's into tit twisting and playing rough."

With this revelation, I poured the coffee over the cups' rims. Owen then exacerbated the flooding with milk. Walking back toward the piano, we slurped coffee from our saucers. I told Owen I couldn't sing in the dark and pointed to the drapes. He said, "I'm a New York bad boy without genius. I hate light. But go ahead."

I flung them open, one after the other. Sunglasses not withstanding, Owen shielded his eyes. "Don't ever shoot big stuff, guy, and try speeding your way free of it."

I opened the last set of drapes to a flat tar roof corralled by TV antennas and ugly chimneys. Raising the window, I got a rush of marinara sauce from a kitchen fan.

"What's it doing out there, guy?"

Above the antennas floated the miasmal haze of an atmospheric inversion. "Dying."

"I despise boys with tans. Where'd you get it?"

I told him I lived at the ocean with my girl friend and my dog.

Owen exhaled cigarette smoke from his nose and mouth, alternately. "I was at the ocean once, guy. Took me two hours by subway, then a bus. When I got there it was raining. My idea of a gentleman's vacation is a solid week on hard drugs in your own home."

I turned back to the window. A pigeon drifted onto an antenna and revealed itself to be a piece of paper.

"The lure of hard stuff, guy, inheres in its initial rush, which feels not unlike a spinal orgasm terminating in a nova of brain bliss. In my younger days I had this thing for hyperventilating until I passed out. The smack rush is the most perfect re-creation of that turn-on I've since found, though coke shot directly with a blast of amyl nitrate comes close, very close."

I turned. He was lighting a new cigarette from the old one. "I've got about fifteen songs, Owen."

He relinquished the piano bench to lay on a sofa, staring at the ceiling, while I reviewed my dubious *oeuvre*. One time, thinking he'd fallen asleep behind his shades, I paused between songs to stare out the window into the sultry haze. Naturally, I wondered how I could have reached the point of desperation where I would entrust myself to an androgynous drug addict with a penchant for unconsciousness.

Owen said, his arm over his eyes, "Write this down, guy," and ticked off a new chord progression for "Ashes to Ashes." After I'd replayed it, he said, "Guy's melodies must be mellifluous and sublime, while his lyrics disarm and portend. It's a new kind of mordancy that will make guy king of the discs."

This went on until late afternoon. Owen honed my musical review to seven songs and recommended I perform them again in a specific order. "I know my musical gigolo is beat, so super manager is offering him top-grade toot on the house to keep him going and going."

I thought, what would Dennis think? and made myself another pot of coffee and smoked a couple of Pall Malls. This did not dissuade Owen from blowing several rails himself. By the time I'd finished, Owen was as ebullient from the coke as from anything I might have accomplished musically. He jumped up, skipped to the window and performed a bongo solo on his head. "Guy is going to get there! Owen promises!"

Then he told me of his friend, Kid Johnnie, the publicity minion at Utopic Records, who had agreed to come hear me play at JP's. "He's our stairway to the A & R people, guy! Our ticket to ride!"

Well, I was twenty-five, with nothing to show for it. I'd been a precocious kid, and failure didn't seem in the stars, which made it difficult of late to look at my hands late at night and believe they actually belonged to me. And of course there was Leah, whom I wanted back and without whom I was less than half of what I wanted to be. This seemed to demand I recapture my lost sense of esteem. This seemed to demand I stick with Owen Chance.

"If Johnnie believes your music's got vinyl in it," he said, "then he'll get us to the A & R boys. That's a promise from him to me."

"I'll believe it when the various inks dry."

"What your super manager wants to do next, guy, is assemble a backup gaggle of musicians to embellish my gigolo's sound. I'm talking about quality people, but ones I can afford."

I was tired and wanted to go home, and said so.

"Fine," Owen said. "Go home, guy. Prepare yourself to assault the notoriously impossible NYC musical jungle."

He disappeared into the bedroom as I loaded my guitar. He reemerged with a camera slung over his shoulder, a set of lights and a full-length mirror. He leaned the mirror against the wall, then told me to sit at the piano and stare into the glass. I did, with a mixture of ennui and mischief, and he flashed several quick ones.

"My wife's performing campy feats with a rich girl who hates men. Torrey calls these flings 'dirty weekends.' I'm all alone."

When the film ran out, he followed me into the street. "Look, guy, I'm just a club manager with a fetish for pop rockers, but I rate one hundred an hour to abuse myself before cliques of dysfunctional leather queens. What I'm trying to say is I'm not in this to make big bone or rip my guy off. Does guy *comprende?*"

I stepped into traffic and fingered a cab. "All too well, Owen."

We shook hands.

"Stay in touch, guy."

The island was in dusk. The entire enterprise was clearly deranged, but my ambition of initiating a culture frenzy of questionable value impelled me more virulently than ever. After all, the meter was running.

THAT NIGHT I WALKED ALONG THE OCEAN BEFORE STOPPING AT Leah's house. A light shone in the living room, but no one was home. I stepped inside. The place was a mess, though the floor appeared finished, and in the corner where the lamp was burning, I spotted Leah's manuscript, *Speciesism.*

From the introduction:

"Speciesism" describes the belief that we are entitled to treat members of other species in a way in which it would be wrong to treat members of our own species.

I turned over a large chunk of pages:

O. S. Ray and R. J. Barrett of Pittsburgh University gave electric shocks to the feet of 1,042 mice. They then caused convulsions by giving more intense shocks through cup-shaped electrodes applied to the animal's eyes or through pressure spring clips attached to their ears. Unfortunately, some of the mice who successfully completed day 1 of training were found sick or dead prior to testing on day 2.

I returned outdoors, counting the ways I loved Leah. The katydids were droning hymns for the mice. I was on number 7 when I spotted her on the hood of a Fiat. She was wearing a white swimsuit with a sweat shirt tied around her shoulders. Her long black hair was dripping wet. "Hello, you," she said.

I touched her hair. "What happened?"

"Swimming."

"Alone?"

"Yes."

"Where's Mr. Howard?"

"Drinking."

"We used to drink," I said softly.

"We used to do lots of things." She looked down the street. "How's the book coming?"

"It makes me sad." She held my hand but still didn't look at me.

"Leah?"

"I'm twenty-five and feel so old."

"I don't know if this helps," I said, "but I love you at least seven different ways."

"I guess," she said sympathetically, "I'm waiting for the eighth, right?"

I hopped beside her onto the hood. "Would you say you still love me?"

"As I love all wild creatures."

"In that case, would it be permissible if I slept in your new home tonight?"

She turned to me and put her arm around my shoulder. I buried my face in her shoulder, which was wet from her wet hair.

We ate breakfast together the following morning at a little place on the beach. Afterward, they buried her father in a private ceremony, which I did not attend.

II

I WAS SANDING A FINAL COLUMN BEFORE PAINTING THE PORCH.
From an upstairs window Rundgren proclaimed that we were
each moving toward a place where our body was not invited.
I stopped everything and stared mournfully into the daylight
filtering through the trees. Two flies, apparently fornicating,
alighted on the column at eye level.

Grandma would have killed them. I, less ethnocentric, allowed the two of them to take off in a flying fuck of wingéd
ecstasy. Then the phone rang.

I answered, "Sorrentino's Funeral Home. Every seven seconds someone needs us."

"Is that you, dear?"

"Mom!"

"Are you on hallucinogenic drugs, dear, or just being what
you imagine to be funny?"

"Righto!"

"Well, I'm just fine, thank you, dear. I've been through the
Scripps Clinic and they're convinced I'm a case of hypo-
glycemia and menopause. I'm feeling so very much better,

though no one in my family seems to care. I'm on vitamins and a special Aireola raw-food diet. I'm walking five miles a day and swimming and drinking coconut milk. I'm attending sensitivity-training lectures with other men and women on the joys of separated and divorced life. Next week we're going to a national park to take off our clothes and touch each other. Are you there, dear?"

"I'm here, Mom."

"I'm feeling much better and I hope you have stopped screaming and arguing and drinking bottle after bottle of alcohol. Are you there, dear?"

"Here, Mom."

"I've consulted with a lawyer about a divorce and bought a shiny convertible. I intend to liquidate stocks and bonds which I originally planned to save for my children but have decided to use on myself to buy a condominium and pay for my psychiatric sessions, a face lift, a new wardrobe and my shiny new convertible. Hello?"

"Hello, Mom."

"Have you found a job yet, dear? And is anything new between you and Leah? Has Grandma been unable to assume the practical burdens resulting from my absence?"

"Actually, Mom, everything's about the same."

"I wish you would write to me, dear. No one has written to me thus far, though Grandma calls and calls and pesters me about when I'll return. Last week—"

I placed the phone on the arm of the sofa and went to the door. Dennis, nude, stared through the screen. Something dead in his mouth, and hairless, turned out to be a mannequin hand. When I opened the door, he repaired to the bathroom to drink from the toilet, leaving the hand at my feet. To him, of course, the toilet is not a toilet, but a drinking well into

which one or the other of us occasionally does his or her
business.

"—I've sent the complete list to your father, who I'm sure
shall covet every last piece I've listed and haggle endlessly with
me about each and every one of them. It's men like your father,
dear, who make lawyers so necessary."

"List?" I said.

"For the moving people, dear."

"People are coming here to take furniture?"

"I'm afraid I'll need it for my new California home. You
haven't broken or sold any of it, I hope?"

"What will *we* do?"

"That's something I can no longer afford to worry about."

"I wish you would, Mom."

"I did—for thirty years. The thought of trying again gives
me blinding headaches and diarrhea."

"I wish you'd come home, Mother."

"Why, dear? Do you like to see me unhappy? Because I'm
not unhappy out here. I'd say you should come out and see for
yourself, but there's really no point. I'm quite sure this is for
the best, and so does my psychiatrist, the people in my sensitiv-
ity class, my sister and her friends, not to mention her new
husband, Orlando. Everyone agrees with me and I know that
you do too and that anything you might say to the contrary is
another one of your canards. In any case, I've got to rush off
to see my aerobic dance teacher at the Women's Center,
where I swim with other women and take massages. Good-bye,
dear. Thank you for calling."

The phone went dead. Dennis stepped into the room,
mouth dripping, and leaped onto the sofa. He took a pillow
into his mouth, growled and started shaking it wildly from side
to side.

A mind reader, Dennis.

AT TWILIGHT, AT THE SEVENTH CHIME OF THE CHURCH BELLS, an ivory-colored Fiat driven by a woman zoomed past the house.

I descended the ladder. Dennis was drinking paint from the rolling pan. I said "No!" and started for my girl's place.

On my way I spotted my father's Avanti for the first time in a week. I looked to the third floor, where a blue light emanated from his room. I went inside and climbed two flights.

His door was open, and on the far wall between two long windows overlooking the sea, a pornographic film was approaching its denouement. The formation was complicated, involving three creatures, two of whom were male, though one possessed hoofs. Seated naked before the exhibition—the horse and young man simultaneously ejaculating—were my father and Splendid Hedgeson.

I closed the door of the menagerie before audience comments could be exchanged.

From the sidewalk I took stock of someone's backyard flowers—orange day lilies, white asters and giant red zinnias. I inspected the house before stealing up the driveway to pick them. When I placed the bouquet to my nose, someone knocked at a window. I turned in alarm. The woman's hair was in curlers and she was waving her finger at me. Despite the closed window I heard her scream.

I ran off; all the way to Leah's house. A blue pickup was parked in her driveway. Leah and someone—a man, naturally —were sharing a Marlboro in the cab of the truck. The pack was displayed on the dash. I watched the smoke diffuse through the open windows and leaned in his side. "I'm looking for Leah Summit."

"Do I look like her?" When he laughed I counted the missing teeth.

"Lumber Lee," Leah said, "this is my neurasthenic ex, Tramp Bottoms."

He pointed past my left ear. "I'm next door. Thirty-one years come Christmas. Lumber Lee Fields."

We shook hands. He squinted at me, or frowned. "George Custer had hair like that. So did Buffalo Bill."

I said, "I'm planning to add my name to America's Hall of Fame."

He opened the door and climbed down. "Let's hope not. Meantime, I got stolen property needs unloading."

I let him pass and climbed into the cab. Leah was on her way out. When I offered her the flowers, the closing door nearly smashed them. I must have cursed. She turned and leaned through the window: her gray eyes, the suntan, that long black hair.

"Hello, Leah."

"Lumber Lee and I found seven sections of porch railings in a dumpster behind the renovated Marina Hotel. Don't you think it would be nice for you to help?"

"I think you are nearer to God than I am."

Leah's tenderness begins in her eyes and rinses downward. "You are a lovable fool."

I reached her the flowers again. "These are for you."

"Forget-me-nots!"

"Asters, actually."

"I meant asters." She accepted them with both hands.

Lumber Lee was piling the railings against the side of the house.

"Let's help," Leah said, her nose in the flowers.

When we finished, Lumber Lee consulted his wristwatch. "Mrs. Fields is expecting me at the laundromat."

I thought, watching the man drive off, that's something I

would like to say about Leah someday and be happy about it.

My girl draped her arm around me, the flowers dangling, consequently, by my right shoulder. We went inside like this, leaving the door open. Storm clouds had covered the sky, and the wind, funneling through the doorway, smelled of impending rain, of the ocean, of summer. The earth almost seemed like home again.

The downstairs was empty, except for Leah's desk, and our footsteps echoed in the emptiness.

"Too bad we sold all our furniture," I said.

"A lot's too bad," she said kindly. She filled a jar with water, inserted the flower stems and put it on the window ledge. Her back was to me. Sometimes just looking at her long legs, the way they rise into her, leaves me dizzy.

She pointed through the window. "Eliot gave me a bird feeder as a housewarming present."

I said, unnecessarily, "I gave you herpes once, remember?"

Leah turned and leaned against the sink, her hands gripping the sides. She was wearing her cutoffs and gypsy high heels; her blue sweat shirt was faded and full of holes from years of washing. "What happened between us, Tramp?"

I lowered my eyes and it began to rain. "I honestly don't know.

"Think."

I did my best. Outside, through all three windows, it was grayness and rain. "You are a woman, Leah. I'm still trying to be a man. Everyone rushed me, even you."

"Ever since I've known you," she said, "I've considered you a man."

I turned away and went to the doorway; watched it rain.

"Speak to me, Tramp."

I wanted to face her, but couldn't. "The thing about failure is how I see it reflected in the eyes of people I want to respect me."

Around the time the cyclone kicked up in the street, I felt Leah's arms slide around me. At least I thought it was a cyclone. Everything began to whirl and I felt myself going away.

Leah said, "I've made you faint. I'm sorry."

I CAME TO IN THE MORNING, IN HER BED. LEAH'S FRECKLED back was to me. I arranged her long hair over my face and peeked at the window. Sun slipped through the bamboo shades in thin horizontal lines. To the right of the window Leah had tacked a photograph of her balancing on my shoulders while I balanced us on a garbage can: my favorite picture. I grasped her close. She moaned and rolled over, burying her face in my chest. "You were just tired."

"How did I get up here?"

"Eliot and I carried you."

Her eyes were closed and I pulled her eyelashes. "You should never allow Eliot Howard to set foot in your bedroom."

Leah placed her hand on my mouth. "I also think you were nervous about tonight."

"Tonight?" I mumbled.

She looked up at me through all her lovely hair. "The ad in the *Voice* says you're playing at JP's tonight."

I don't think Leah saw the terror that flared in my eyes; I simply pretended I was massaging them to wake up. As for the subsequent moaning, this would best be attributed to Leah's own kind of massage.

Basically, when she feels good about us, Leah will come with the dreamy and langorous peace of a rainbow returning to earth in a slow dissolve of nacreous dust.

Mine, though less poetic, is nonetheless the only resurrection I know.

In celebration I prepared Leah a cheese omelet with rye toast and Irish coffee and brought it to our bed. I kept her company with a rock 'n' roller's antistress breakfast of iced vodka and lemon and two ten-gram Valium.

III

FROM THE PORCH ROCKER GRANDMA INQUIRED WHERE I WAS
going in the white linen pants and jacket. When I mentioned
the JP's gig, she said, "How come I ain't never been invited?"
I kissed her good-bye and told her to ask Leah. Then I hauled
my Gibson and amplifier off the porch. Grandma followed me
to the street, where I loaded up the Avanti.

"Sonny," she said, "let me cut it a little," and held up the
scissors and comb from her apron pocket.

I readied my hands defensively. "Really now, Grandma. I'm
warning you."

"But they won't let Sonny in the door of any nice place
without no shirt collar and hair like that."

I pulled the *Voice* advertisement from my pocket and
showed it to her. Grandma moved her lips while reading.
When she finished, her eyes fixed on me in bewilderment.

I said, "You see, Grandma, I'm paid to look this way. It's
my job. I've got a manager and a backup band in the works,
and I get half the door at five bucks a throw."

Grandma was intransigent. "But you don't look normal,

sweetie. Sadie Fischgrund thinks you look like a drug dealer."

I got into the car. I snapped my only extant demo tape into the deck and blasted Bottoms out the death-seat window. Grandma winced, as I imagined the A & R men had done in the past. I blew her a kiss and drove off. In the rearview mirror she seemed a frail old lady holding a pair of scissors the size of hedge clippers.

I DROVE TO LEAH'S HOUSE. LUMBER LEE FIELDS AND HOWARD Eliot were seated on cinderblocks on the porch. The sun was fading in the west and the windows behind them glistened with copper light.

"Where's Leah?"

The way they shrugged in unison, I thought I'd asked them the meaning of life. For my part I was far less terrified of the insolubility of *why* we live than of the gruesome exigency of *how to* live. For example, the answer to *how to* make it as a singer/songwriter seemed a magic act in comparison to the question of *why* be one.

Sometimes, I'm afraid, fear is assuaged by drinking beer and driving fast, so I gunned the Avanti down Main Street toward the parkway entrance. Passing Shafto's Exxon, I saw the crimson flashers in the mirror and heaved the beer can into traffic. The voice on the loudspeaker said, "Pull it over and keep your hands on the wheel."

I am a citizen of a crumbling empire. As a nation we spend too much on armaments; our industrial equipment is obsolete, our production off; inflation has become an endemic worm in the heart of our gluttonous system. Everyone is nervous, especially the authorities. Fearing for my ass, I did as instructed.

Reflected in the Avanti's rearview mirror, James Tunnel—

known affectionately as Lincoln—hitched up his belt of deadly weapons. My window was open.

"If I can screw you, Bottoms, I'm gone to."

"Linc, look it—"

"I want your license and I want your registration. Furthermore, your insurance card. What I don't want is lip. I'll count to ten."

"Lincoln, I've got an important engagement—"

"I hear lip!"

"Goddamn it—"

"I'm at seven already and you haven't followed one instruction." He rested his hand on the riot stick.

I reached into the console between the front seats and culled through a mess of papers. I handed Lincoln the requested material.

He said, "Shit. The registration's expired two years and the insurance card's a year worse than that." He frowned. "Consider yourself nailed. Where's your license?"

I found it stuck to an expired library card in my wallet. Lincoln pointed to the expiration date thereupon. "June of seventy-seven!" Now he smiled. "On behalf of the Township of Avon, I'm proud to announce your ass is under arrest. Step out of the vehicle."

"Lincoln—"

"Officer Tunnel said step out!"

I obeyed. He moved me aside and leaned into the Avanti.

"You got drugs on your person or property?"

"Look, Lincoln, I've got to be in the city in two hours to perform at a club. I'll do anything to get there." I laid my fraternal hand on his shoulder.

He straightened up and stared at me. "You got that spaced-out pupil dilation. Let's take a look-see in your trunk."

"I'm just nervous, Lincoln."

He eyed my hand. "Remove your person from the officer."

He searched the car, top to bottom, and found nothing but cigarette stubs. Naturally, the Republicans passing by in Chryslers presumed me *guilty* and scowled. Lincoln had collected the butts in his hand.

"We'll get the lab-test results tomorrow. We find marijuana or cocaine laced herewith, it won't get you sent away, but I'm shooting for a probation ruling where I can keep my eye on you." He smiled. "Now, how about your person?"

"Cut the shit, Lincoln!"

"Put your arms on the roof and spread'm."

"No way."

"What!"

"Lincoln, I've got the biggest musical break of my life tonight and you can't do this to me." I got into the car.

"What the hell you doin', Bottoms?"

I slammed the door. "Leaving, Tunnel."

He reached for the Smith & Wesson .38. "Go on, please. Try it."

I looked up at him through the open window, my epitaph reflecting in his sadistic black eyes. "Lincoln," I said sensibly, "you've been a bastard to everyone in this neighborhood since you were ten. You're not well-endeared and you've never been steadily paired. So there are more people than you'd care to know about willing to agree with me if I begin a campaign regarding your suspected gayness."

Tunnel's face tightened. "You calling me homo?"

"All that matters is the innuendo, Lincoln."

"I ain't no *homo*, mister!"

"I hate to think how your father and his friends at the bar will take it."

Lincoln glared. I could see his brain snag in his eyes. He pointed down the block. "Say you'd struck down a pedestrian child back at the school zone. How'd you feel now about something like a homicide perpetration all over your bumper?"

"I swear to God, Lincoln, I'll never do it again."

"You ever, *ever*, say anything to my father, I'll shoot your brains right out your face. Backwards to front, you got that?"

"Lincoln—"

He pulled out his gun and pointed it at my nose. I held up my hands in surrender.

"Now you repeat after me: 'Officer Tunnel is a damn good cop.'" He screamed, "Say it, Bottoms!"

I did.

"'Who ain't no way a homo.'"

I repeated this verbatim.

"Now," he said slowly, "who's the asshole here?"

I pondered this, finger at my lips.

He went berserk. "Who! Who! Who!"

"Me. *Me!*"

He composed himself and returned his weapon to its holster.

"You're in big trouble, friend!" Thereafter, he returned to his cruiser and shot off, as it were, down the block.

When I passed him two blocks away, my hands still trembling, he had already apprehended another citizen: an old black man in a license-free Bonneville with a sticker on the rear bumper.

> JOIN THE ARMY
> TRAVEL TO EXOTIC
> DISTANT LANDS: MEET
> EXCITING, UNUSUAL
> PEOPLE
> AND KILL THEM

So much of life is spent thinking of nothing; the mind refusing to confront our simple Holocenic mess and evanescence. I broached my mortality in silence while racing past the oil refineries bounding the Cancer Alley flatlands of the Jersey Turnpike. To the south the lights of Manhattan's skyline rose into a lethal twilight of sorrel and copper pollutants, while to the east of Jersey City's detritus, the Statue of Liberty ushered in the darkness with a fiery hand job.

Not long afterward I lugged my guitar and amp into JP's on fashionable First Avenue.

I entered, as is my wont, with something less than insouciance. In fact, I stood in shock before what seemed a crowd of standing-room-only proportions. The telephone rang and I heard the bartender say, "Tramp Bottoms." I turned to listen. He repeated my name into the receiver, enunciating carefully above the din. Then he shouted, "Jesus Christ, *Tramp Bottoms!*" and hung up. I stepped to the darkest corner of the bar. I set down my equipment and inquired who was playing tonight. The bartender closed his eyes dramatically. "Tramp Bottoms," he whispered.

I was upset too and ordered an inexpensive beer with which to wash down a high-milligram dosage of Valium.

As my slow slide from the world began, Owen emerged from the smoky crowd in a swish of turquoise glitter. He disappeared as quickly, all solemnity, moving my equipment to the platform, where he performed his usual routine of endless dickering. Then he looked into the crowd and tapped the mike twice. "Guess who just showed up!" Someone whistled and Owen held out his arms in a crucifixion stretch to model his sequin shirt. "I'm a rhinestone cowboygirl," he said.

The place was paneled with mirrors and in one Owen was talking to a body with purple hair. It appeared to be a man. Someone abruptly kissed my neck. When I turned, Torrey Chance put her full weight into me. She was wearing a black dress and a black headband; moreover, her black eyes were encircled with black eyeliner. The woman undoubtedly possessed a black heart and a witch's black tongue.

"I'm in black," she said, "and you're in white. I know tricks that will leave you sore."

I told her I didn't speak Manhattan. She took the beer from my hand and stuck her tongue into the bottle's amber throat. Then she handed me a gold box wrapped in red ribbon.

"Owen has a hunch that your pet peeve is bad girls who play games. Happy birthday."

I told her it wasn't my birthday.

"I like to play games one at a time. You've got a very cute Italianlike ass which leaves me helpless. Open it—the box!"

I found it filled with nothing but silvery packing straw. "I don't get it."

"I've got Mandrax, Lemmons, Percodans. Pharmaceuticals. No counterfeits, promise. After the show I want you to do me all night. Okay?"

I was about to make a run for it when Owen grabbed my arm. "Kid Johnnie," he said, "this is Tramp Bottoms."

Kid and I shook hands. He wore a black vinyl jacket, open, and no shirt. His hair was marcelled and purple.

"Tramp here," Owen said, "is a super-nice, super-good-looking guy who stupidly sold his wa-wa pedal, right?"

I aspired to be duly incoherent. "In those days," I said, "I was idealistic."

"Before I learned the true meaning of bullshit," said Kid Johnnie, "I played for Buddha and the Percolators. Ring any bells?"

I promised they didn't.

Kid Johnnie screamed. This was a laugh. "Oh God, I love it. Love it! No bullshit. Owen hinted you were my kind of cripple."

"Kid Johnnie," Owen explained, "is often obnoxious for a number of sordid personal reasons. For one, he has a record of juvenile delinquency as long as my fetish list."

I nodded.

"I do hope," Kid said seriously, "that you make a lot of quick bone for a discerning record label. Be it Utopic or not is not the question. The question is one of bullshit reality."

I listened to more of the same at a table near stage until an anonymous voice said from the ceiling, "Ladies and gentlemen, please welcome Mr. Tramp Bottoms!" and a blue spot followed me to the piano. I slid onto the bench and lit into "Coastline Crucifixion."

Stand in the shower
For more than an hour
Get high on smoke
The world's a mediacracy joke
So many things have gone wrong
It isn't even funny

I can't determine what's worse
Being goddamned
Or godforsaken
If I'm not mistaken
Like those two in Eden
They both eat it!

You're my only resurrection, baby

The world's too hard on me
So I get hard on you
You got a way of making me soft
I'm only at home inside of you

I eat you but the world can't
There's mass starvation
Fascist elections
It's a miracle I wake up

With an all-American erection
Life makes me so hard on you

It's clear what's in store
People just whore and whore more
They don't age so much
Just get sicker and sicker
You're the only thing I can stomach

You're my only resurrection, baby

Someone yelled above the applause, "Go all night!" and I
remembered how Leah and I once had. "This is the most fun
I've ever had playing with myself," I said, and played "Ashes
to Ashes."

I dreamt you were dead
I held your head
Words were said
Prayers read

Then we gathered
I cried
Couldn't hide
Masochistic me

Dust to dust
God's a broom
Gurdjieff says we die
To feed the moon

Nothing real ever mattered
All our illusions promptly shattered
In one ear, out the other
Far too hopeless to recover

So I reap, you sow
Head to toe, head to toe
Life's a game of 69

The cathedral exploded
I was demoted
Sadistic world
Dead on arrival

I moved to my guitar and settled on a stool. I said, "I don't want much, but what I do want better come true!" and played "Brain-Damaged Heart" and "Crazy for Free." Then I went back to the piano and finished the set with "Entranced," "Driven to Death" and "Rock Bottom."

They applauded as you dream they will. I cried hoarsely, "Thank you!" and stepped from the spotlights.

In the sudden darkness, shaking Owen's hand at the table, I felt all the enervation and sorrow of post-coitus triste. The applause continued and I returned to the stage for the requisite encore. I played my latest, "Wheelchair Twin."

When it really was all over, when the ceiling spots came on and poured down through the cigarette smoke, Owen grabbed the stage mike and announced that there would be a party at his place from one o'clock until the cocks crowed.

The club emptied as abruptly as a premature ejaculation, and I got stuck driving Torrey downtown to Owen's loft festival. I sensed conspiracy.

We followed Kid Johnnie, who drove down Second Avenue in an Austin Healey rust bucket. Torrey sat beside me, her legs enfolded beneath her. She was langorously smoking a cigarette, and the dreaminess of her black eyes bespoke a 'lude high next to none.

"Want to know something, mister?"

"Not especially."

"You remember that dead boy? The one who turned me on like a radio till he OD'd? The one I see in you?"

"The thing is," I said, "I just can't bear to be grossed out all the time."

"Well, the test came back positive."

"Test?"

"I'm going to have it. Want to be a father?"

We stopped at a red light. I needed asylum. Singing your heart out to the unknown and perfidious and then listening to the deranged will not compare to singing hymns and hearing confession. When I pulled up in front of the Spring Street loft, I left the Avanti idling and helped Torrey from the car into an upright position of barbiturate disorientation.

"I told Owen," she said, "that I didn't want him inviting anyone whose face I haven't sat on. You think he listened or what?"

"I'll go park," I said, and watched her wander in the direction of the entrance. She opened the security door and started gracelessly up the stairway, stumbling twice before rising out of view.

I drove down the block, passing a coterie of Bottoms' loyalists. I waved, but they didn't seem to recognize me.

By the time I had parked the car, I was in front of Leah Summit's house. When I cut the headlights, a swarm of moths rose toward the moon.

Eliot Howard was asleep on the porch in a rocking chair, an empty bottle of wine beside him. His arms were wrapped around his chest, his mouth wide open and drooling. Forty years old and a displaced person.

The screen door was unlatched. I went in, located a large beach towel and covered the pathetic bastard. Then I tiptoed upstairs.

All the windows in her bedroom were open. I listened for the ocean but heard only crickets. Leah was reading in bed by flashlight.

"Eliot?" She shined the light in my eyes.

"Eliot!" I lay down beside her. "Eliot!"

She closed the magazine, *Defenders of Wildlife News,* and looked at me. "Hello, beautiful boy."

"Eliot's sleeping on the front porch like a good dog. Have you seen Dennis?"

She pointed to the corner. The terrier was asleep beneath a window, on his back, his legs splayed shamelessly. I undressed, got into bed and covered my face with the sheet and white cotton blanket.

"Good night, Leah." I kissed her naked shoulder and closed my eyes.

She slid her hand beneath the covers and rubbed my chest. "Don't you want to tell me about the show?"

"God, no."

"Are you all right?"

I didn't open my eyes. "I love you, Leah."

WHEN I WOKE IN THE MORNING, SHE WASN'T THERE. DENNIS LAY beside me. I could smell Leah's perfume on the pillow and went back to sleep. When I woke again she was typing downstairs. I just lay there. The morning was merciful with a cool sea breeze that softly flung the bamboo shades into the air and back against the window frame.

There was no song, however, in happiness.

I took a bath; Dennis watched. Then I went down the stairs for coffee, a simple descent into decency that reminded me that one's ego was not a dick and therein should not require the world constantly to stroke it.

As for what Leah and I needed from each other—that was something else again. After a month of separation, it wasn't unlike a refresher course. Naturally I feared the remission might crap out on us. But still, no one questions the ecstasy of drinking coffee with your girl friend in her backyard, her white kimono ruffling open at the knees at ten o'clock on a Sunday morning in August.

IV

THE MIDWEEK MORNING WAS LUMINOUS AND STILL, MORE serene than lonely. I was standing on the penultimate rung of the ladder, rewiring Grandma's clothesline, when the Beach House School van arrived. A column of children paraded down the ramp holding hands to form a long line of round-headed innocence. Teresa followed behind in her wheelchair. The children wore pointed party hats and waited obediently in line for my sister's instructions.

Grandma leaned out the kitchen window to my left. "Superman wants to speak with you, Sonny." She handed me the phone.

"Guy? Super manager buzzing."

"Ah!"

"Shall I explode with super news?"

"Figuratively."

"Kid Johnnie has recommended Tramp Bottoms to Utopic as we had hoped!"

I heard my heart begin to thump and, with my eyes closed, raised my face to the sun. "Yes?"

"And when guy does his thing at Kenny's next Tuesday, there shall be an A & R personage among his fans. We must convince this personage to give us our ticket to ride."

"How far can he take us?"

"There, guy. All the way there."

"A contract?"

"No, guy, but a preamble to a contract. *There* means free recording time with studio backup, compliments of Utopic. But we each know that this shall lead inevitably to a contract. Because guy is a god of rock, and Owen is leading him back to his empyreal home."

I said confidently, "No, Owen, it'll never happen."

" 'Fairy tales can come true,' " Owen sang, " 'they can happen to you *if* you're young at heart!' " He sniffed. "Are we young at heart, guy?"

"Regressively so, Owen."

"In that case, allow me to upbraid my minstrel gigolo for his strategic failure to make the scene at his own party the other night."

"You know how it is after a performance, Owen."

"I'm not sure I do. Unless you're saying you're the type who empties his load and nods out—you know, never says anything romantic afterwards."

"Something like that."

"Guy is wrong. My friends were turned on to you. You owed it to them to appear. Next time they might not be there."

"Owen, I have bouts of sadness concerning a woman."

"Guy?"

"I've got a dripping exterior-surface paintbrush in my hand, Owen."

"I wonder if you realize how fine you were at JP's?"

"I don't."

"Well then, *ciao* now."

I turned to ask Grandma to take the receiver. She was standing at the open window, shuffling the morning mail. "Ain't this funny, Sonny. Here's someone who looks just like you with the name Kenny Castaway."

When I handed her the phone, she handed me a postcard-size snapshot of myself behind the piano at JP's. On the back of the card:

Owen Chance Productions
Presents
More Tramp Bottoms Wizardry
August 13th 10:00 P.M.
Kenny's Castaways

I climbed in the window, contemplating the possibility of happiness for the first time since Nixon resigned, leaving a trail of vomit and prerecorded obscenity.

Grandma handed me a tray of two cakes under glass. I followed her to the Last Resort as obediently as the damaged follow Teresa.

A new sign had been posted on the uncut lawn.

ANOTHER PROPERTY

SOLD

BY

CENTURY REALTY

Grandma passed the sign without batting an eye. I followed her through the building to the pool. Picnic tables with red cloths had been arranged around the pool, and red balloons were hanging heavy as rotten fruit from long white poles. My sister was administering a game of pin-the-tail-on-the-donkey while Carver Bridgeman, the one-armed driver, failed to coordinate a general turmoil of children, who raced around the pool like exotic birds in their pointed little hats. Meantime, my father, in a black tuxedo coat and hat, a fake beard and mustache, performed magic acts behind a makeshift booth. Above us all a cloudless sky, blinding with light.

I set the tray of cakes on the table beside the sandwiches. Grandma said, "For their own sake I hope there ain't no flies," and removed a swatter from her apron pocket. Applause began. I turned. My father was bowing before his audience of the congenitally limited. Watching the wind blow the children's hair into their faces, I thought, what a coincidence this is happening before we each die.

Around then my sister cajoled the water-headed birthday boy to step onto the diving board, and thereafter my father, taking up the violin, led us in a happy birthday salute to Gary, who found it rather difficult to maintain his cool and bounced ecstatically up and down on the board, his little hands covering his ears. When the applause quieted, Grandma betrayed the sandwiches and the stampede commenced.

I trailed my father into his hotel office, which was filled with costumes. He exchanged his top hat for a headdress. "Sit'm down," he said oddly.

I did. Then I asked about the Last Resort.

My father lit a cigar. "Condominium people were very generous, Junior. Daddy's worries are over."

"How much?"

"Enough to discourage me from divorcing your mother. Sometimes, when all else fails, marriage becomes a good investment."

"How inspired of you."

My incurably fat and cynical father removed his coat, shirt and pants and hung them up. "Truth is, Junior, the day-in and day-out isn't supposed to be inspiring. I'm not about to throw away thirty years of marriage for lack of inspiration with six figures on the line!"

He turned his back to me to apply red-and-white bars on his cheeks; I watched his heathen face in a square little mirror hanging on the wall.

"Now you hear me, Junior. No matter whom you are with, no matter under what conditions, no matter where you might be with them or why you are with them, life is always and always will be one big mess of emotion in which we are each all by our lonesome. You read me?"

"I do," I said. "And you're wrong."

"Only thing I've ever really been wrong about is not insisting I've always been right."

I stood up to go. My father's eyes were upon me in the mirror. "What will you do with yourself," I asked, "now that the hotel's gone?"

He turned around, his face completed. "Thirty years ago your daddy thought he might become a writer. He gave it up to run his father's hotel after his father retired to Florida with Grandma and enough money to buy a house and a fishing boat. Between me and you, the thing that probably killed him was how his son ran the place into the ground in the span of his father's retirement." My father drew on his cigar. "Be that as it may, what your daddy's going to do is write himself a novel and smoke his White Owls on a tropical beach."

Standing pathetically in his boxer shorts, he examined himself, adjusted his headdress and picked up a bow and arrow. "Let me pass, Junior. There are children in this world who still love me."

When he got outside he broke into native American war woops and cries. The children, their mouths filled with cake, screamed for more. Through the window screen I watched my father shoot his arrows at the effigies of America's three most recent Presidents.

Children simply loved the man.

I NEEDED TO THINK. WALKING HELPS. OUTSIDE THE RESORT, TWO people were kissing in the back of a yellow Dodge pickup. A portable radio the size of a refrigerator boomed this message: *"Friends, I'm not ashamed of my Christian belief that the world gets better and better only when we each try harder and harder to make it that way. Let's you and me put our faith in Jesus on the line today and support the Republican party person of our choice who's dedicated to putting a lid on inflationary tendencies. Friends, we'll be helping ourselves!"*

I continued down the street. The lyrics to "Seven Kinds of Loneliness" just dropped from the trees. I was humming a chord progression when Leah Summit drove past in a foreign sports car. The white reverse lights flashed as she backed up.

"Eliot and I just received a tip on exotic old tubs for sale. Tonight we're going to Manhattan."

I didn't understand the connection and admitted as much.

Leah said, "Eliot wants a friend along when he meets his wife. She wants to see him again. Isn't that nice?"

Eliot sat in the death seat, his head bowed. He was picking nervously at the cuticle of his thumb.

I said, "Howard, remarry already and move back to Manhattan."

He didn't move a muscle. Leah admonished me with a furtive nod of her head.

"I'm joking, Eliot."

He lifted his eyes to me. "I'm sorry; I was thinking. Would you mind repeating your question?"

The mental-health-club sticker on the visor was in full view, and I thought, there but for the grace of Ms. Summit go I. "Eliot, I just hope you and your son and your wife work things out."

He smiled mournfully. For a moment I thought he was going to cry. He opened his mouth to speak, but couldn't.

"Eliot," I said. "It is cake. Cake!"

"Cake?" asked Leah.

"A piece of cake. You know, a cake walk. You know, *cheese.* Cheesecake!"

"What is?"

"Getting back together."

She closed her eyes a moment, then put the car in gear. I grabbed a slant of her hair. "Wait!"

She kept her foot on the clutch pedal. "Now what?"

"Would you have dinner with me at a restaurant tonight?"

"I'll be in the city, remember?"

"Late," I said. "We can eat very late. New Jersey as Italy."

"Let go of my hair, Tramp."

When I did, her foot let up on the clutch pedal. She waved to me in the sideview mirror and I waved back, standing in a fog of Italian auto exhaust.

I RETURNED FROM TEN MILES OF RUNNING AND COULDN'T WAIT to dig into one of Grandma's thirteen-course dinners. The note, however, said that Grandma and Teresa had gone with the children to see *Lady and the Tramp.* Dennis watched me shower. Then he would neither leave my side nor take his eyes off me. When the smell of the neighbor's dinnertime barbecue left him drooling, I got the message. I don't believe that the one and a half cups of dry Discount Chow was what he had in mind, but I was in no mood. Eliot and his fucking wife! "Eat the shit, damnit!" I screamed, and Dennis raced, terrified, from the kitchen.

On the front porch I ate a grilled cheese sandwich and cold beans from the can. Further, in the bottom of the sixth, the Yankees were trailing Baltimore four to one. The radio crackled with each flash of heat lightning, but the illuminations made the sports section easier to read in the dusk.

Meanwhile, the Castaways postcard featuring my sorrowful face blew off my lap in a gust of wind. Dennis glanced up from his cheese-embellished chow, pounced after the card and kept right on going.

I am nearsighted, but I squinted and made out my father riding his bicycle unsteadily up the road toward the house. He was wearing his white bathing cap and black goggles, but was naked below the neck. Dennis charged into the bicycle and my father went straight to the macadam. I charged into the road myself. My father lay flat on his back, reeking of booze.

"Daddy?"

He opened his eyes. Then he smiled. "There once was a man from Calcutta who played with himself in the gutter. The tropical sun beat down on his gun, and turned his glue into butter!"

"Come on, get up and come inside."

"There once was a man named Dave, who kept a dead whore in his cave. You must admit it smelled like shit, but think of the money he saved!"

When I attempted to get him to his feet, he cried, "Don't you hurt me! Don't you hurt me!"

I thought, it has happened, and ran to the house for a bathrobe. By the time I returned, it was too late. Lincoln Tunnel, his cruiser's lights flashing, stood at my father's side. When he saw me come down the steps he drew his revolver: "Halt! Police!"

I kept going and offered the robe to my father. He stared at me, then at Lincoln, before declaiming, "Yet McGruder was shrewder and screwd'er!"

Lincoln packed his .38 and withdrew his nightstick. "Mr. Bottoms, children live on this block. Get up now on a voluntary basis or I'll have to kick your ass."

"Take it easy, Tunnel," I said, and received the point of the nightstick in the solar plexus. I went straight to the ground.

Tunnel screamed, "I said *up, mister!*" and poked my father's head with the stick, then hauled him into the rear of the cruiser.

He tossed my father's bicycle onto our front lawn. "You get up too, else I'll be forced to make you."

Dennis and I stood obediently at the curb and watched the cruiser race away.

V

THE MOON CROWNED THE TWIN CHIMNEY OF THE LAST RESORT.
I heard Grandma's voice and went inside. She was nowhere to
be found. On the TV, however, an elderly woman resembling
Grandma soliloquized to the nation. I sat on the sofa to listen
and spotted a letter.

Dear Teddy,
    I'm sure proud of my boy. I won't never forget the first day I
baby sat for you and how you always was so nice to Mom Bottoms
when you got older. I had to make a new life for myself with my
son and his family after my husband Hodge died after 52 years of
marriage. Now again I am trying to make a new life with my
grandchildren—Teresa, a crippled girl who works with retarded
children, and Aldo Huxley, who is handy around the house.
    My family is very good to me and I have a clean room with a
bath and nice food. I cook a lot and watch TV. I love to read and
my granddaughter Teresa gets all the good books from the library.
I want to read your books but don't know how to get them. I am
sure we will like your books, even if they are about family's that
ain't happy. I'm sure proud of you. I can't realize you are grown
up now. I think of you as my boy and I guess I always will.
    God be good to you, Teddy.

                                                        Love,
                                                Mom Bottoms

I put the letter aside. Grandma came from the kitchen carrying a teapot, cups and cookies upon a tray.

"I got us nice coconut cookies, Sonny. Go see if Daddy would like some."

She set the tray on the coffee table and turned off the TV; easier said than done at eighty-eight. I, for example, might have folded the family laundry in the same amount of time. Then again, it had taken me twenty-five years to accomplish nothing.

Grandma sat beside me on the sofa. "I only watch if there ain't no one here, sweetie. I ain't never been good at loneliness. It scares me."

I said, "Ditto for me," and routed a cookie to my mouth.

"I seen you done a beautiful job on the porch," Grandma said. "Sonny looks wild, but he's a good boy." Meticulously, she poured two cups full of tea. Then question marks wrinkled around her eyes. "Sonny, why does people like Daddy and you try so hard to be unhappy? It's like you two forgot about what is and ain't important."

I took the teacup from her hand. "Speaking of Daddy," I said calmly, "it's nothing serious, but he's in the hospital. He took too much sun and fainted." I sipped the tea to buy time. "We can see him tomorrow."

Grandma was perplexed. "Too much sun? I bought him that nice sombrero so he wouldn't get sick." She looked forlornly from me to the steam rising from her own cup. "Daddy just ain't been right since Mommy left. He won't say nothing, but he can't do without her."

Her hands began to tremble, and she had difficulty withdrawing the photograph from the envelope that lay beneath her letter to Teddy. The photograph was a black-and-white shot of a young woman dressed in white shorts and blouse, seated on a lawn, surrounded by flowers.

Grandma said, glancing from me to the photograph, "That's Mommy. Look how happy she was. It ain't right for this to happen after thirty years with us. I ain't said a word till now, see, but now I'm mad. Either you or Daddy got to go out there and get Mommy."

I reminded Grandma that Sonny was terrified of flying and that her son was in no condition to travel. This cynicism brought the woman to tears.

"Life ain't something you always like doing, sweetie. The world's not good no more because people only do what makes them happy. I love you, but you're wrong about things."

Well, she'd had it with me. Before I could defend myself, she retired to her bedroom. I fed the cookies to Dennis, put the cups in the sink and went to my own room. Something in the saxophone elegy of Pharaoh Sanders' "Memories of Lee Morgan" sent me tiptoeing down the stairs to apologize to an old woman who had participated in a long line of disastrous begetting. When I peeked into her room, she was folding clothes into a suitcase.

"Grandma?"

"You mind your business, see!" She came to the door and kissed my forehead. Then she locked herself in.

A PINT OF JOHNNIE WALKER RED SELLS FOR $5.23 AT MAIN Street Liquor and Wine. I had eight dollars to my name. The next thing I knew it was two dollars and change. I wandered to a house owned by a woman I'd known in my past.

Half a block off I could hear her typewriter clacking. I stared through the window. When she looked up she gasped in horror.

"Sorry," I said.

Something jumped into view and stared at me face-to-face

through the screen. Its head was orange and black wool and it sported eyes like Dennis'.

"You bought a dog!"

"I'm afraid I found her in Central Park when I was waiting for Eliot."

I put my nose to the screen and the terrier licked the wire mesh.

"She was running in the street with no collar," Leah said. "An Airedale. Are you drinking out there?"

"Come see."

"Can't. Working."

"Why so late?"

"Because I'm interrupted and interrupted."

"May I come in?"

She sighed. "I'll come out for just a second."

She sat with me on the porch, the terrier eying us through the screen door. "You drink all that by yourself?"

"You take the rest." I handed it over.

Leah stared at me staring at her.

"I am changed," I said. "Really."

"You just want my advance money."

"Also your body."

She drank an impressive amount and didn't flinch at the swallow.

"How'd things go with weirdo and his wife?"

"*You* can call Eliot a weirdo!" She drank again. "He's staying with her tonight. I came back on the train with Lucy in a box. How can you drink that stuff straight?"

I showed her how.

"Why get drunk, Tramp?"

"Sadness. Also, Daddy's in the hospital."

"My father's in the grave and I'm not drunk."

This did me in. I held on to her hand and recited my list of the thousand natural shocks that flesh is heir to.

Leah said, "Drunk boy's getting sloppy," and went indoors. By the time I was on my feet, she had the screen door latched.

"Hey!" I shook the door handle. "Hey!"

"I have work to do."

"What'd I do now, Leah! What the hell did I do!"

"I have *deadlines*!"

"We all have deadlines!"

She began to type. I gazed inconsolably through the screen door. The Airedale was lying on her stomach, face on her front paws.

"You think she and Dennis will get along?"

"That's not the problem. Thanks for dropping by."

"Well, bye."

"Bye."

"Bye, Leah."

"Bye, Tramp."

"I'll be going now. Night."

"Night."

"Leah?"

"I love you, too, Tramp."

I went home, erratically.

THE NEXT DAY, WHEN I PEERED INTO HIS HOSPITAL ROOM, my father was seated at the side of his bed, his back to me, playing solitaire. Beyond him was a wide wall of windows full of sunlight; in contrast he was as dark as a silhouette. I glanced stealthily over his shoulder; naturally, he was cheating. He said, without turning to me, "I'd rather go to jail without bail than submit to another honey-and-lemon colonic."

I sat facing him. He needed a shave and a haircut, and the rumpled pajamas augmented the impression of derangement. He glanced into the windows' brilliance. "No more magic in screwing, Junior. Sunshine leaves me cold. Sick of myself. Beer's gone. No point."

"Just take it easy."

He frowned. "Don't remember a thing. Doctor said you did this to me."

I rendered the nasty facts as best I could, and my father blew his stack. "Don't you sit there and tell Daddy he was naked on a bicycle on Third Avenue, USA!"

"The truth, I'm afraid."

He stepped to the door and closed it, then returned to the bed. "Who else knows about this?"

"Lincoln Tunnel."

"Tunnel! I'll have Walker Mills have the mayor kick that little bastard's ass into the unemployment line!"

"You were drunk and naked. Don't blame Tunnel."

My father closed his eyes. "Now hear this, Junior. Daddy was on his way to the beach for a swim when Lincoln Tunnel ordered him to remove his trunks. Walker Mills saw it all, saw everything, as did Daddy's son, Aldo H. We comprehend one another?"

"Lying isn't necessarily one of my vices."

I watched him lay back on the bed and stare abjectly at the ceiling.

"They got Daddy for drunk and disorderly, Junior. Mayor phoned this morning. Advised I comply with the county health people and all charges will be dropped."

"You need help," I said. "Face it."

"Seems I'm forced to, lad. County people have Daddy on a one-week juice-fast-and-honey-enema routine. Also, two five-mile hikes per day. Guaranteed to keep us away from alcohol. There's five of us. When the week's up we submit to two months of therapy. It's legal now. I signed the papers this morning."

I sat there watching him breathe, his stomach rising and falling. He closed his eyes and didn't move a lash. I heard traffic moving on the road below us.

"Splendid Hedgeson phoned me yesterday," my father said. "Told me she could count on her pinkie the number of orgasms she's had with a man inside her, and that one was a fake. In a word, Daddy's been discarded."

"Don't," I said emphatically, "relay this smut to your son."

"Point is, Junior, your mom and I need to talk."

He must have opened his eyes, because as I was leaving the room he called, "Where do you think you're going!"

"Out of my mind." I continued on, passing an orderly wheeling an enema bag, which dangled from a metal hanger, into my father's room.

Halfway down the corridor, I heard my father exhort, "Physician, heal thyself!"

WHEN I RETURNED TO THE HOUSE GRANDMA AND TERESA WERE waiting on the sidewalk, glaring.

"We thought you was sleeping!" Grandma shook her head.

A horn beeped behind me. I turned: a cab.

"How did you expect us to see Daddy if you weren't here to drive us?" My sister was not happy.

I lowered my eyes shamefully. "I forgot."

"Selfish, Sonny!"

Grandma rolled Teresa to the curb. I opened the rear door and took my sister in my arms. Grandma said to the driver, "My granddaughter got in a horrible accident last year. She don't eat meat either and teaches retarded children. My son had a heat stroke. We want to go to the hospital."

I folded the wheelchair and placed it in the trunk. Then I leaned in the window on Teresa's side. "I'm sorry."

She straightened her pale-blue dress. "Grandma's flying to California to speak with Mommy. Things really can't go on like this. You and Daddy have been impossible."

"Now what."

"It's what you don't do," my sister said quietly, "that makes it so difficult. I'm at work most of the day and Grandma has to take care of everything. It's too much for us."

Grandma, sitting on the far side of my sister, leaned forward. "I can't take so much walking up and down them stairs, sweetie."

I looked defensively from one to the other. "But I rebuilt the front steps and repainted the porch."

"But you ain't once cleaned your room or cleaned them garbage cans," Grandma said. "I been watching!"

"The yard's overgrown," Teresa said, "and the basement's flooded. The sump pump's broken and needs repairs."

I stepped away from the car. "You both sound like Mommy!"

"Don't argue when you're wrong, Sonny. It ain't a nice trait."

My sister nodded her agreement.

"*Goddamn it all, I'm trying to get a record contract!* I'm not the repairman!"

The cabdriver looked over his shoulder. "I gotta start the meter now."

I kicked for the cab as it drove off, but missed.

IN THE PARK, ADJACENT TO THE MONUMENTS ERECTED FOR THE dead of four American wars, Dennis was dogging a French poodle with terrible energy. I envied him this curative pastime. Naturally, I thought of those myriad times with Leah, of her gorgeously freckled back, its particular arching contraction upon climax. Indeed, Leah and I have our tricks, our habits, our repertoire of private methods. Admittedly, they are gathering dust. On the right nights, enhanced by the right pharmaceuticals, our apartment frequently sounded like a slaughterhouse of redemptive passion. Frankly, I am at my best, feel most centered and at home on earth, in those semiconscious, weightless aftermaths of carnal exhaustion. So, undoubtedly, do many other men and women, which explains better than anything the regrettable side effect, overpopulation.

The old man on the bench confessed that the two had been going at it all morning. Exiting the park, I trusted that his cheap thrills would remain vicarious.

The sign on Leah's door read: KINDLY LEAVE SUPPLIES IN CARRIAGE HOUSE. DO NOT DISBURB BEFORE 1 P.M.

I peeked in the window. Two columns of books on Leah's desk and a typewriter, but no typist. An asparagus fern, newly purchased and glistening in sunlight, hung above her desk. Eliot came to mind: He's bought her a plant and now she's fucking him! I circled the house, spying in every window. When I entered the backyard I discovered a man and a woman embracing.

Leah said, "It didn't work."

I cried, "You didn't think some flimsy note would send me away, did you!"

"Eliot's meeting with his wife, *you jerk!*"

"I am sick to death of Howard here crying on your shoulder!" I picked up a rock the size of a hardball. "Run, Eliot, run!"

He didn't move.

"He's having an anxiety attack!" Leah said.

Eliot stepped away from her. Tears were visible in his blue eyes. "I'm sorry. I'm a wreck. My wife's pregnant from a man half her age and plans on having the child. She told me this over roast duck—after we'd made love."

"You *ate* a *duck*!"

"Let go of him!" Leah cried, and yanked me away by the hair.

Eliot Howard put his hands to his throat. Leah said, "My God, Tramp, can't you help for a change?" She was furious.

So was I. "Look, Summit, if he needs a friend, I know a woman who needs someone as much as he does. She loves sports cars and helping the damaged, and the only possible inconvenience to Eliot is that her legs don't work anymore."

They were both staring at me incredulously. When I reached the driveway, I turned back. I screamed, "I'm getting Dennis!" and cleared the hell out.

FULLY CLOTHED, I STOOD IN THE OCEAN AT CHIN LEVEL, FACING the waves, for two hours. When I went into the family house, I was dripping saltwater and didn't give a damn. I walked through the living room and the dining room before I reached the kitchen. When the water dried, a trail of white salt stains would mark my thorny path. Tough.

On the kitchen table a vase of five daffodils supported Grandma's note.

Dear Teresie,

A friend of Leah's, Mr. Coward is driving me to the airport. Sonny never showed up. Mr. Coward is the one who left you these beautiful flowers. Men used to do this all the time before life got the awful way it is. It's only right you should be nice to him. Please keep the house nice and clean for Mommy, and don't let Dennis or Sonny mess things all up.

Love,
Grandma

Next to the note was an envelope addressed to Teresa. There wasn't a stamp or postmark. I boiled water in the teakettle and held Eliot Howard's letter over the steam. The flap pulled free of the glue in one piece. I read by available light.

Dear Teresa Bottoms:
 As you know because I told you that day that Leah's father died, my name is Eliot Martin Howard. You should know some other things. To be exact, I am forty years old. At one time I was married to a very nice woman named Eileen. We had a son named Skip. From time to time something is not right with my mind. In the past three years I have been institutionalized more than once. The worst is over now though, I hope. My wife is remarrying soon and I am cutting back on medication.
 Lots of times I'm inexplicably afraid of things. But I am hopeful that you will agree to have dinner with me sometime soon and allow me to explain myself better.
 If you don't mind, I will come by for your answer? If you are mad because of this letter, then I'm very sorry, and didn't mean anything by it.
Your friend,
Eliot Howard

I resealed the letter and propped it against the flowers. Outside the kitchen window Dennis was asleep on his back, his rear legs splayed, his weeny's sheath no doubt burning to a crisp. I opened the window and the terrier rolled his head toward the sound. For him everything was indeed upside down.

"Mind your instrument doesn't get a glazing, lad."

He yawned langorously.

In the attic, on the Wurlitzer electric, I composed "The Whole Earth Is Our Hospital."

THE DOORBELL SIGNALED BELOW. I DESCENDED THE STAIRWAY staffing the chord progression of "Whole Earth" on a piece of sheet music.

A man stood before the screen door. "Telegram for Mr. Tramp Bottoms."

I unlocked the door. "No one says that anymore."

"Mailogram for Mr. Tramp Bottoms. Happy?"

Opening the envelope, I thought, something has happened to Mommy; something has happened to Daddy; something has happened to Grandma.

REHEARSAL TONIGHT WITH MUSICIANS OF MY CHOOSING. CALLED AND CALLED. AWAIT YOU. COME AT ONCE.
CHANCE.

I phoned. The message on the recorder captured Owen's effeminate rasp. "This is the voice of Owen Chance, manager of rock stars of all ages. I'm in rehearsal with the Tramp Bottoms Band. Tramp is the future, only now. Catch him at a club near you." Then the screech of tires and the sound of a car smashing into a wall before the beep tone cued the caller's message. I do not, alas, speak via machines. I hung up to look for keys to the Avanti.

WHEN THE BUZZER SOUNDED, I TRUDGED UP THREE FLIGHTS. The door inscribed SPRING STREET STUDIO, was ajar. My song "Ashes to Ashes" was winding down in a punkified guitar finish à la the Pretenders.

Owen introduced me to his musicians: Wes Fast, bass; Kris Hoomes, lead; Max Marx, drums. Max wore a ten-gallon cowboy hat and shades, green cowboy boots, a T-shirt with DON'T

TALK TO ME, I'M MUTE printed on the front. Wes Fast stood shirtless, wearing eye makeup, tight pink pants, yellow tie and his own black hair. Ms. Hoomes was strikingly androgynous with crew cut, red sweat pants and clogs, a mauve T-shirt and little red-and-green beads around her neck.

"The arrangements," Owen conceded, "aren't precisely you, guy, but sit by my side and we'll deliver our rockified translation."

I sat beside Owen at the keyboard. The others stood on the platform littered with empty pizza boxes and coffee cups.

"Kris and I arranged these numbers while playing with my syncopator," Owen explained, and my alleged band lit into "Coastline Crucifixion," featuring Hoomes and Fast in a hardcore guitar counterpointing interlude. When they finished, Owen explained, "Rearranged to demonstrate guy's New Waveability."

"I hear Talking Heads," I said. "I don't hear *me.*"

Kris Hoomes turned to Max Marx. "The sixteenth bar goes into a five-sixths then back to three-sixths," and they played "Driven to Death" with heavy metal hostility, punctuated by Owen's rhapsodic and ethereal Minimoog solo. Afterward, Owen said, as if to an imaginary audience, "Tramp can be hard and full of sexy stridency, or Tramp can be soft and seductive," and they ran through the tender side of the Bottoms' oeuvre.

When they were through, I said, "You don't need me. Bye-bye."

Owen grabbed me at the door. "It's simply our interpretation. Now we're going to Trampify the entire show to your satisfaction."

"Show?" I said. "You're not thinking of us for the Castaways?"

"My God, yes! This band represents Owen's latest strategy in guy's meteoric rise from lonesome to stardom."

"Forget it, Owen."

He said, slowly, "Guy, guy, guy."

"No!"

He lit a cigarette. "We simply must musicalize the gigolo's show. We need to dress his lyrics in sizzling rhythms and arresting melodies."

"I am *not* a *rocker*, Owen."

"God himself is a rocker, guy! Are you greater than God himself?"

"You're not playing my music."

"Believe me, guy. Your manager understands to the very marrow of his urban bones what the Utopic A & R people want. Call it inside info. Call it feminine intuition. But don't call it bad names."

"In the first place," I said, "we haven't enough time to plan a show."

"Time is all we do have, guy. Time and space. And me: Chance. It happeneth to each of us, guy." He nodded to the piano bench. "Sit down. Take some blow, let your fingers flow." He held a vial of coke at eye level. "Blade's on the kitchen table."

I said, "Just coffee," and went through it song by song with the band. The music had so much electric drive that my mordantly rueful compositions were transmogrified into deranged and nihilistic anthems. Owen's refrain throughout was, "Guy must believe in super manager's acumen. Guy must be trusting." Toward the end of rehearsal, as he noted my increasing anger, the refrain changed to, "Guy must go for record-contract megabucks. Talent must marry commerce to have its day and say."

I suppose I didn't protest as much as I once might have. I was aging every second and getting nowhere fast. Ultimately, I'd rather be a fool with a vocation than a fool with squat.

AFTER WE BROKE I VOLUNTEERED TO GIVE OWEN A RIDE UP-
town. Twice he glanced at his watch and said, "God, she'll kill
me, too."

I made the mistake of expressing my curiosity.

"This is a long story, guy. But to make it short, right around
now Torrey should be coming un-anesthetized upon her abor-
tionist's rack."

I stopped before a brownstone in the fashionable East Sixties
and waited in the car.

When they came out Owen was holding Torrey's hand. She
was wearing baggy designer jeans and a white sweat shirt with
the words LIVE ON TOUR WITH THE DEAD splattered above and
below her chest. Her black curls fell prettily to her shoulders,
though the dark wraparound shades demonstrated her prefer-
ence for the depraved.

They got in the car, she in front, beside me; Owen in the
back.

"If I could stand on my head," Torrey said, "it'd feel like
a sore throat." Then she appealed to Owen. "I'm ravished and
I'm wounded. Take me someplace garish where I can be
happy."

I drove downtown.

The city is hot and loud. It is unclean and unsafe, it bustles
with frenetic people as excretion buzzes with flies. Basically, I
wanted to settle down in a place green and enduring; I could
teach children to play the piano, teach them guitar. I could
help Eliot Howard build things. I could avoid certain vulgari-
ties inherent to my trade.

At Twenty-seventh and Second Avenue, Owen told me to
pull over.

"I'll park and meet you inside," I said.

When the restaurant door closed behind them, I took off

like the sky was falling, thinking, if only I could move toward the light with the same avidity with which I flee the darkness.

HOME IS WHERE WE GO WHEN THE WORLD IS TOO MUCH WITH us. Home is where we begin respectably, where we want to end respectably. In between we must be satisfied to pay and pay and pay.

I went indoors. On the stove smoked a wok full of snow peas and carrots and onions. Eliot Howard, facing away from me, was tossing the vegetables gracefully in the metal cavity. My sister sat reading a book at the kitchen table, which was set with chopsticks and little handleless cups.

I tiptoed away and got as far as the living room before stumbling over something. Leah had kneeled to greet Dennis and I'd gone right over her. She dusted me off. I took her hand and brought her to the front porch.

"My editor wants a thorough rewrite. I'm in trouble."

I whispered, "Let me eat you out."

"*What!*"

"Take you out to eat, I mean."

"I was invited to eat here."

"But I think something's happening in there."

"Something?"

"Between *them.*"

"Well, let's hope so."

"Now, about us."

"What about us?"

"That restaurant we loved when we were very poor and very young."

"You treating?"

"I will, if you pay. Incidentally, I'm pleased to announce that I'm fully trained and that you can now quit breaking my balls."

"I don't think so, Tramp, but I'll let you know when I do."

"I swear to God, Leah. I am ready to back into adulthood."

"You're not even close to ready. Sorry."

I studied her, troubled. "Are you positive?"

"For example, I may have to leave you for quite some time, and I don't think you can take it. Can you?" After a moment she added, "You see!"

I had gone white as a sheet. "Leave me?"

"To get the book done."

I asked for amplification and got it—right between the eyes. It seems that Leah and her editor had agreed that *Speciesism* was suffering from the distractions of her tenuous living conditions. The editor had recommended a coworker's summer home on the southern coast of Spain, where she could work peacefully and inexpensively.

I laughed. Then I smiled. Then I screamed: "It's just an excuse to get rid of me for good. I know when I'm being dumped!"

Leah didn't say anything. I trailed her off the porch.

"Who is he, Leah? A matador? You've met a matador in Manhattan and now you're going away to fuck him ten times a day! Right? *Right!*"

Leah had scooted to the side of the house. I had my hand covering my eyes when the kitchen door slammed behind her.

I wouldn't have eaten stir-fried vegetables for all the tea in China.

VERY LATE THAT NIGHT THE BEER MADE ME CONFESS THAT I wasn't close to trained. I crawled in next to her. The sheets were cool and smelled like her hair.

In the morning I sat in the sun beside Leah's new garden of flowers and herbs. Lucy was following two steps behind Dennis. When he stopped to mark the fence, she sniffed a rock and got her head pissed on.

Leah could be heard in the bathtub.

Well, I fell to my knees, imploring the angels to spare my ass and Leah's from premature ruination.

Lumber Lee didn't know what the hell I was doing. "Today's starting time for your wife's bedroom deck. How is she—decent?"

"*What!*"

"Clothed, son. Clothed!"

I just kneeled there, visibly addled.

"My boy Jack and me needs to pile support beams right where your supplication's taking place. You best tell your wife about our starting."

I got cautiously to my feet and went inside to my wife. It felt nice—pretending, I mean.

The terriers watched Leah and me make waves in the bath-tub. Outside, the world carried on inexorably, as three billion members of our bewildered species performed one kind of flying fuck or another at an incessantly rolling doughnut. But for the moment, with Leah and I engaged in hot congress with the shades drawn, within a four-legged tub of carcinogenic water, I felt happily apart from, and simultaneously a part of, the world.

THE FIRST PERSON TO CALL ON LEAH'S NEW PHONE WAS my sister. She told me to come home at once, thus giving my morning some direction.

A tricyclist passed as I neared the house.

"Hey, Merrill!"

"Up your rear with a rusty spear!"

I placed my hands around my mouth for volume. "Fuck you, Miller!"

"In your face with a can of mace!"

Out front, Eliot Howard was cutting the lawn.

"I was going to get to that, Eliot. Really."

"I don't mind." He smiled. "I love the smell of cut grass."

Teresa waved from the porch, rocking in Grandma's white wicker chair. I tried to remember the last time I'd seen my sister in short pants and a halter top. When I closed my eyes to elicit a memory, Scotty was standing beside her.

"Mommy's sending Grandma home today," she said. "You'll have to hurry to meet her flight." She tossed me Eliot's key ring. "Also, there's a letter in today's mail from Mommy's lawyer. I want you to read it before I show it to Daddy."

A rumbling issued from the street. A green van the size of a football field turned the corner and pulled to the curb. The driver waved a yellow piece of paper. "We come fo' the furn'-ture!" He handed me the yellow sheet from Coast to Coast Van Lines.

"Right inside," Teresa called.

I turned to her, perplexity evident on my face.

"Mommy wants her antiques," she explained. "That's also in the lawyer's letter."

"What about us?"

"I think this is easier than arguing, don't you?"

I watched the two men climb from the cab. Eliot, entranced with the effort to cut the lawn in even rows, seemed useless.

"You want me to stick around, Mrs. Bottoms?"

"Why?"

I nodded xenophobically to the two gentlemen walking toward the porch, and Teresa frowned reprovingly. I removed myself to the Fiat.

"What about the letter?" Teresa called.

"I can't read lawyer," I shouted, pulling out.

VI

GRANDMA HAD A PRESENT FOR SADIE FISCHGRUND. I DROPPED her next door and then carried her bags into the house.

At the base of the stairway, Teresa's empty wheelchair blocked my upward progress. I pushed it aside as the grandfather clock tolled portentously three times.

It was after I'd tossed the suitcases onto Grandma's bed that I first heard the tremolos. I stepped into the hallway. The door of the guest room was closed.

I will confess this much: Ever since the doctors had reported that she was incurably crippled, I had wondered whether this would prohibit her from ever again achieving, say, post-orgasmic easement. My genuflection brought my eye to the level of the keyhole.

I squinted for a second.

Tiptoeing away, I felt privy to my question's answer.

I knocked out "Crippled Lovers" in no time.

I WAS LOADING MY EQUIPMENT INTO THE FIAT WHEN LEAH turned the corner on roller skates. I opened my arms and she sailed into them. My arms closed reflexively when she kissed me. Then I held her away, looking at the only woman I have ever loved. "We grew up on this block."

Leah glanced around. "I fell in love with you before I knew any better."

"Lyrically speaking, God wanted it that way."

"Practically speaking," she said, "I've got work to do."

"I myself have a rehearsal with my new band."

This is the sort of specificity that Leah digs. "Drive me home. I want to hear everything."

The ride in the convertible lasted three minutes. I hadn't even begun when Leah started from the car. "Come back after your rehearsal for cognac and the exciting conclusion of your story."

I grabbed her arm. "Guess what?"

"You've got one minute."

"Eliot and Teresa made love this afternoon!"

Leah nodded calmly. "It isn't the first time."

"*What!*"

"Bye, *you.*" She hopped out and closed the door.

"Wait a minute!"

"Yours is up." She moved off.

I stared through the windshield, trying to figure it out. When her screen door slammed shut, I snapped out of it. I glanced at the gas gauge, got out of the car and rapped her knocker. She was on her knees in a turmoil of papers when I stepped inside.

"The puppy's gotten into my manuscript!"

"I need money for gasoline."

Leah put her face in her hands and fell flat on the floor. The Airedale was hiding beneath the desk, her tail thumping nervously against a chair leg. I said, "Nice play, Shakespeare!" and she charged across the papers into my legs. Leah screamed, "My book!" and began to moan.

Pagination took the two of us an hour, and I had been late

for rehearsal to begin with. Leah's phone rested on a stack of books in the corner. When I removed the receiver, the books crashed to the floor. Leah didn't even look up. She stuck her fingers in her ears and stared at the manuscript on her desk.

Outside the window three birds were feeding at Eliot Howard's contraption.

Owen answered on the first ring. "Just where the fuck is the leader of our band!"

As innocent as Mickey Mouse, I said, "Owen, my girl friend had a problem. She needed me and I need her more, I'm afraid, than I need you."

"My guy's career is a problem! I have him and his band booked at Lewis Friedman's Snafu tomorrow eve. I'm dishing out favors to orchestrate this last-minute preview—all to make my guy a minstrel gigolo in super-fast fashion—and now guy is royally fucking up!"

"Owen," I said, "I think we're experiencing our first failure to communicate."

"Guy is fucking with his rock fate and with his manager. This means God might just dump him in the rock graveyard with other pretty boys who forgot how far away the world of vinyl truly is."

I was duly penitent and consented to rehearsal at the Spring Street Studio no later than noon the following day.

I hung up and turned to Leah. Her blouse was off; she was staring.

"Thank you for helping me," she said tenderly.

SOMETIMES LEAH AND I SLEEP HEAD TO TOE. WHEN THE PHONE rang that morning, I woke in a welter of ankles. In ten years Dennis had never once jumped from bed to answer the phone. Leah did, and poked me in the eye with a polished toenail.

" 'Lo?" After a pause, she added "Oh boy" and handed me the phone.

"Daddy's disappeared," Teresa said.

I sat up. "At last!"

"He left the hospital without permission."

"I'll tour the bars."

"Looking for Daddy?"

"Of course."

"Eliot's already out driving around."

"Runaway-dog strategy?"

"What?"

"I say, how is Eliot?"

"Fine. I've never met anyone like him before. Bye."

Leah had my ears in a leg lock when the phone rang again. I groaned "Stop, Leah" and answered as best I could. Naturally, I couldn't get the phone anywhere near my ear. When I finally did, after pinching Leah, my head was ringing from the pressure.

It was Grandma. "Daddy got away so he could go for Mommy. He just called us from the airport. Helleww?"

Leah decided to get sexy.

"I'm here, Grandmaahh!"

"Helleww? Sonny?"

"I'll come over, Grandma."

"Don't come alone, sweetie. Come with Leah."

Leah was applying avocado oil.

"We'll do our best, Grandma."

VII

WE FINISHED REHEARSING LATE IN THE DAY. OWEN AND MAX
Marx lost the draw and cabbed the equipment to Snafu. Kris
Hoomes, Wild Wes Fast and I walked to Chinatown for an
MSG-rice high. On the way uptown we picked up a pint of Old
Grand Dad to facilitate digestion.

Snafu offers green peeling walls, a formica bar as ominous
as an operating table, half a dozen crooked tables with un-
upholstered chairs. Above the stage, glowing in the dark at the
far end of the narrow room, the announcement LIVE SHOW
TONIGHT in orange and green iridescence.

We each did hope so.

From the jukebox the vitriolic Clash vilified the queen's
fascist regime to the delight of the single paying customer who,
though without an instrument, pantomimed a guitarist gone
mad on diet pills.

Owen escorted us to a backstage area that in better days had
been a kitchen and not a drugstore. I leaned against a doorless
refrigerator while the others lit up in three crumbling chairs.
A wall in an advanced state of decay supported a wet mop
reeking of ammonia. Above us, two improperly connected

fluorescent tubes emitted flickering blue light. "This," I said, "is what my mother's migraine must look like," while Kris Hoomes and Max Marx proceeded to orally simulate a guitar-and-drum riff.

Time spent backstage is what drives musicians to hard drugs. The crowd out front was small. I counted fifteen heads before walking through the darkness on Owen's cue. When I hit the keyboard the pink spot caught my crotch, then moved up to my head. "The band got stuck in traffic, but I'm Tramp. This is 'Driven to Death.' "

I walked down to the sand
The last dry spot of land
Leaned my head in my hands
And prayed for a pop 'n' roll band

Oh, we race around
And we make one-way love
Pound for pound and in and out

We try to keep clean
Look for God in between
Each other's legs
In our beds we lose our heads

Baby, I'm an Un-American dope
At the end of my postindustrial rope
I can't keep on keepin' on alone
My heart needs you like my dog
        needs a bone

Race around
In and out, out and in
Between our legs ain't no sin
It's a place to bury our heads

I don't pretend to be smart
I'm a loser in a low-life art
So's your Daddy
He's gone to hell
In a carbon monoxide Fairlane
He did it to kill the pain
Living's not life till it drives us insane

I owned up that I was a confused kid in need of a nation of fans, and mixed everybody up by singing Boudleaux Bryant's "Love Hurts." I was in the mood.

Wes Fast joined me on bass for "Ashes to Ashes." Then Kris Hoomes and Max Marx drifted out for "Coastline Crucifixion," a straight 4-4 rocker hinting at the epoch's nihilistic breakdown into self-absorption. Meanwhile, the spots flashed pink to purple in blinding alternation. I'll say this much for Owen—the audience seemed to go for his arrangements in a bigger way than they went for my heartache. When the applause subsided I introduced the band and we launched into the acidly strident "Rock Bottom."

After all, ten songs. Then you walk offstage, your head humming with the latest melody line. If the audience knows you, they clamor idiotically for more. At this one no one knew us. Still, we came back out, leaping to the stage. I spoke confidently into the silence, "OK! OK! Thank you!" and ignited the band into "Very Tramp" with a hot guitar riff. Then we called it quits.

After the show we hauled the equipment off the stage to make way for the Urban Boys, hailed a cab and began loading. Owen sat in front with the driver, the others in back. My manager took my hand through the open window.

"Tomorrow is tomorrow, guy. Tonight is tonight. Tonight my guy was good. Tomorrow he cannot afford to be good; he must be irresistible. Tomorrow is Armageddon. After tomorrow there will be no tomorrow. Find your desert, guy. Meditate there. *Bon soir.*"

Technically, there are no deserts in New Jersey. The beaches, however, are barren with sand. I took a blanket and an extra sweat shirt with me. I explained my decision to Leah in her bedroom. Dennis eavesdropped at the foot of the bed. Leah wished me well and slipped her dress over her head. I took in the silvery underthings and decided to join her.

Reaching to light the blue candle on the night table, I read, in the match's momentary flare, the spine of *A Spanish Grammar Primer.*

Breakthroughs

I

TERESA TEACHES, LEAH WRITES, GRANDMA COOKS. ELIOT BUILDS
to keep from falling apart. I make music in my room to hedge
against making trouble in public.

I stood at the attic window, facing the horizon, strapped on
my Fender Mustang, plugged into the Pignose amp and enter-
tained the entire block with a riff of Hendrix's "All Along the
Watchtower."

When the phone rang I assumed it was an appreciative
neighbor or perhaps the police calling to express the community's gratitude. "It's my dog and his stoned friends," I answered. "It won't happen again."

"Junior?"

I paused. That voice. "Daddy?"

"I asked first."

"Where the hell are you?"

"In yet another state of confusion."

"You've been drinking!"

"At the Mark Hopkins, actually. In San Francisco. I'm looking out the window at Alcatraz."

"How's Mom?"

"There's a phone at my side. Every time I call she hangs up."

"She has her reasons, in spades."

"No doubt she has. One time I wouldn't speak with myself for a week. What matters at the moment, however, is not kicking your mate's privates when he's down and out."

"Have you apologized?"

"Apologized?"

"Apologize to Mom at once!"

"I thought of candy—but it'll melt in my hand, not in her mouth."

"I've said it twice now."

"I'll call back, lad. Fare thee well."

I switched from the piano to the guitar to the piano, rehearsing the ten-song Castaways set. I possess amulets: a one-armed Buddha, a pink plastic Jiminy Cricket, a rubber cow the size of a child's hand. I kneeled before this trinity and prayed that certain things come true. The phone rang again.

"Maybe you can make heads or tails of it," my father said.

"Go," I said.

"Daddy's just completed a long talk with your mother's sister. I told her to tell your mother that her husband wanted to apologize for conduct unbecoming a spouse."

"Smart move."

"This got Junior's mom to the phone."

"Don't stop now."

"She said she welcomed my apology and would have to consult with her psychiatrist before accepting or not. In any event she categorically refuses ever to return east."

"Well," I said, "the shack's burned to the ground, the Resort's soon a pile of rubble and the house is less than half furnished."

"She thought maybe something by the water out here. Then

she refused to see me for at least two more weeks. This got me to thinking of Mexico. Ruins, castanets, cliff diving."

"No cliff diving!"

"Take time to figure out what I want from your mother."

"Say your wife!"

"Your wife."

"*Your* wife."

"Meanwhile, you show them your stuff tonight. Grandma tells me you've got a big show."

"You wishing me luck?"

"I've always wished my boy luck. It breaks a father's heart to see his boy unhappy."

"Too bad the boy's father never told the boy that."

"He's telling him now."

I looked at the amulets. "Better late than never, I suppose."

I WAS ON MY WAY OUT THE DOOR, SURFBOARD UNDER MY ARM, when the goddamned phone rang. Grandma was outside hanging wash. I watched her small arms stretch toward the sky, her hands full of clothespins. Conceivably, a person could die hanging a blue handkerchief.

"Bottoms here." It was my mother. "I've just spoken with your other half, Mom."

"I'm sure you'll agree, dear, that your father represents my very worst half."

"Listen, Mom, I'm trying to get to the bathroom. My pants fly at half mast and I'm holding my breath."

"I do want you to know, dear, that I'm terribly thrilled about Daddy's call. I can't see him, however, because my eyes are all black-and-blue from the face lift. When Grandma was here I lay in bed with cold cream on my face until she left. The lift is just our little secret."

"Oh well," I said. "My face is turning blue and I don't want to soil the parquet."

"I do hope you'll visit me in California before I grow old and crippled or too senile to remember who you are and what you want from me. For I shall never again return east. It's so depressing there—the deterioration, the minority groups. The fruits and vegetables are so fresh and colorful here. The weather's nice. I'm ever so much happier."

"Cramps, Mom. Cramps."

"I'm afraid your father will have to change a very great deal, however, if he wants me to remain his companion. He's not a bad man, just a terribly thoughtless, egocentric one. We've done it his way for thirty years or more and now it's my turn to have a say. Fortunately, I have a marvelous sense of humor, otherwise I shouldn't be at all confident that the marriage could go on."

"Flies, Mom. Flies."

"Incidentally, dear, did I mention to you that I'm putting the house up for sale?"

"What!"

"I'm afraid I have no choice. But if you'll excuse me now, I'm late for my yoga class. Don't let Dennis on my bed."

"Your bed is gone. Why are you selling the house?"

"You just be nice when the realty people drop in. I'll let you go now, dear. Good-bye."

RECUMBENT UPON THE BOARD, MY FACE TO THE SUN, I ROSE and fell to the waves' rhythmic assault. My eyes were closed and I was picturing three amulets. Please, I prayed, do not let me fail, hate myself, drive Leah away for good.

Anxiety lifted me to my feet. The wave broke sooner than I anticipated and caught me rising from a squat. I was thrown head first over the board—the ankle strap yanking free—and surfaced with a mouthful of sand. I was coughing, fighting my way blindly through the surf, arms flailing desperately, when someone grabbed me and helped me ashore.

Eliot Howard said, "You looked in trouble. I hope you don't mind me rescuing you."

I spit water and sand from my mouth. "Indebted, Eliot."

"If you don't mind me saying, you've got a bit of kelp caught on your nose."

I blew my nose in my hand and cleaned my fingers in the surf. "Anything else?" I looked down at what resembled a jellyfish—a condom full of seawater.

"I'm looking forward to your show tonight," Eliot said. "So are the others."

"What others?"

He pointed up the beach. I squinted: a blue blanket, two beach chairs, an umbrella; Grandma seated, Leah and Teresa on the blanket.

"You left an invitation on the kitchen table. Teresa showed it to us days ago."

"I don't want anyone to come!"

He put his arm around my shoulder. "Leah's packed some cold beer. Have one, you'll feel better."

We approached them in tandem.

Grandma was asleep under the umbrella in a white bathing suit and white beach hat. The umbrella's circular shadow, dark as antimatter, seemed a way out; I stepped into it. "Am I still here?"

No one replied, each privately transfixed.

Sometimes the world goes silent and motionless as a painting: Grandma on the beach in white, alone in her dreams; Teresa and Leah playing Scrabble; Eliot Howard kneeling for a beer and casting a long shadow against a sand castle; Tramp trapped inside his head.

Leah had spelled "uxorious" vertically and was counting up

an astronomical sum—all this in her peerless black mesh bikini that left nothing to the imagination. Teresa was in red, pale as an English girl. The way she lay on her side, you would've never guessed she was crippled.

Leah glanced up at me, her cinnamon-colored body glistening with oil. If heaven is a place, it is surely a woman's body.

"Some spill we had," she said, and resumed adding her score.

"Our suit," I answered, "sends all the boys for a tumble."

"Too bad I only have eyes for you."

"Don't be cross," Teresa said. "We're sure you'll do well tonight."

I looked at them all. "Please don't come. Anyone!"

Sharply, Teresa whispered, "Grandma's sleeping."

Eliot handed me a beer. I popped the aluminum top and sprayed myself in the face. Teresa bisected "uxorious" with "exigency" for a triple-word score. Chugging the beer, I acknowledged that I couldn't compete with these women.

Eliot moved beside me with a can of his own. "We thought," he said cautiously, "that you might drive in with Leah in my car. The rest of us could take your father's."

"No!" I sat beside Leah and watched. She spelled "bore" using the first *e* of "exigency."

"In case you've forgotten," she said, "you are a *performing* artist."

"Please," I begged. "I'm too nervous. Maybe the next one."

Eliot handed me another beer; apparently the first was dead.

Grandma, stirring in her sleep, muttered, "Not a hospital," and commenced to snore.

I hoisted the can into the sky. "To Howard and my sister!" I drank with my face to the sun until the well ran dry. When I opened my eyes, I noticed the chagrin in their averted faces.

Leah reached across the blanket and squeezed my nose.

"Feel that?"

"It's only my second!"

"Mick Jagger and I," Leah told them, rising, "will be in the water."

"Don't you ever call me Mick Jagger!"

"Gustav Mahler and I are going for a sobering dip."

We held hands down to the water. I can be a petty person, grasping and paranoid, and in this manner inspected the suit. "My girl and Martin Luther: They both stand revealed."

The water reached our ankles. Leah snatched the beer from my hand and executed a perfect karate trip. I plunged head-first into the churn of seashells and sand. When I surfaced, Leah said, "We *are* coming tonight. Did I hurt you?"

II

BLEECKER STREET IS A CARNIVAL STRIP OF NOISE AND NEON, OF sidewalk eateries, multiracial canaille collapsed in doorways, unisex boutiques, sex joints with plastic and rubberoid aids erect in window fronts and, of course, clubs: the End, Village Gate, Castaways. In short, one more concourse of mercantile jetsam to commemorate our national failure of checks and balances.

Leah told me to shut up for once.

The Castaways is narrow, long and gloomy. Opposite the bar stands an idle consumer's trinity: pinball machine, cigarette machine, jukebox. Further in, where the place opens up, sit a dozen tables; beyond the tables a stage and piano. On the stage, of course, stood Owen Chance, my fastidious and possibly deluded manager. He was testing equipment, complaining about lighting, the positioning of the piano, the air conditioning.

Leah and I took a drink at the bar. When I introduced her to Owen, he said, "This man will do for rock what Fizzies did to water. Watch and see."

Leah was in white, as was I. Owen wore regally loose black pants and shirt. His eyes were lined, a ring hung in his left ear and his hair was newly coiffed. I left Owen and Leah at the bar and stationed my guitar and amp on stage. Owen cried, "You're fucking with my set!" and repositioned my equipment. I placed Jiminy Cricket, the buddha and the cow on the piano top, facing their mendicant's seat. Leah winked from the bar. I winked back.

"I have done everything minus you," Owen said. "You have done everything plus me." He began testing the spotlights.

"I'm too scared to think," I said, and joined the band backstage.

When I came out to ask Leah to wish me luck, the house was filled with fans. Torrey was sitting with her at the table closest to stage. I went over to them. Torrey was saying, "My shrink tells me I'm an addictive personality. Are you on the make or what?" Leah smiled at me.

"Torrey," I said, "this is my . . . this is Leah Summit."

Torrey leaned forward, taking Leah's arm. Her problem, I'm afraid, was drinking and pill-popping: the Quinlan combo. "Owen is bi," she said, "with submissive quirks; I'm bi with a pref for rugged girls with oral gifts that go all night. Now tell me about you."

I beckoned to Owen. When he came over he said, "Julian is here from Utopic. I've assured him we are on his road to utopia."

"No offense, Owen," I said calmly, "but I need to speak privately with Leah, and Torrey's too high to get the message."

Owen frowned at his wife and then yanked her away by the hair. She screamed once or twice, but settled down after Owen slapped her and handed her a drink. I sat down next to Leah.

"If the music gets too loud," I said, "I won't mind if you stick your fingers in your ears."

Leah had something on her mind. "I've loved you since you were eight, Tramp. You weren't famous then. Famous is what other people make you want to be."

"I'm just saying if it gets too loud, if you don't like it . . ."

Leah took my hand. "I don't think you and I should allow ourselves to be ruined by such an obvious thing."

I thought a moment. Then I said to Leah, " 'Such an obvious thing.' I like that."

When I came out the third time, it was for keeps. The blue spot ignited with the keyboard's first chord and I sang "Crippled Lovers." I acknowledged the subsequent applause with a smile and noticed Leah was surrounded by Eliot, Teresa and Grandma, who waved.

"My grandmother's here tonight; she's eighty-eight!" The place went nuts. Then I played "Driven to Death."

Across the room Torrey Chance was smoking a cigarette in a huddle with Julian, the A & R man, and Kid Johnnie. They were clapping along with the others. The spot went from green to blue and the cigarette smoke seemed to change directions. I sang "Crazy for Free" and "Coastline Crucifixion." Wes Fast joined me on the latter, his red Gretsch strapped into place; all he had to do was plug in. Thereafter, "Kris Hoomes, lead guitar; Max Marx on the bangers. Incidentally, I'm Tramp Bottoms," and we hit them with a lineup of songs more powerful than a locomotive.

Toward the end we went MOR. I dedicated "Entranced" and "Rock Bottom" to Leah, both songs tightly structured four-minute elegies where the melody line is kept under lock and key. Then we finished with "The Whole Earth Is Our Hospital," featuring none other than Owen Chance. For the encore we played "Ashes to Ashes," my whimsical ditty of fear and trembling in an iconoclastic epoch of monogamous ambiguity. I shouted, "Our last and only chance!" and the lights extinguished in an implosion of finality.

About the time Mr. Marx and Ms. Hoomes were employing US currency as a nostril straw to bump up backstage, Owen and Julian, the A & R man, walked in on us.

"Julian Daye," Owen said formally, "is with Utopic Enterprises. He wanted to say hello before catching another act uptown."

Julian Daye was framed in the doorway in his velvet top and snug designer jeans. "Jewel Daye just loved it," he said. "Loved it!" He shook our hands with his beringed left one. Then he lit a cigarette and blew smoke dramatically toward the ceiling. "Why be polite about it?" he said. "I'm in search of simple, effective noise for the teenager horny for headphone kicks. I'm enormously thrilled by the talent I've heard tonight. I'm turned on by it." He looked right at me. "However, I give you fair warning. At the moment Utopic is cleaning house. We'll have to see what's what." He glanced at his wristwatch. "Fuck! Must boogie!"

"We're each thrilled by your attention, Julian," Owen said, and the two of them walked out on us.

Owen disappeared after that. I don't know where he went or why. I sat with the only people who mean anything to me. You know them.

Eliot had ordered two carafes of wine. I kissed my sister first, then Leah and finally Grandma, who said, "You screamed, Sonny—so loud and nasty!"

In the end, I explained to her, we look for a way to pay the rent and finance a night on the town with a small circle of friends with whom we can let down our hair; also a way to redeem ourselves with a woman of at least ten times our quality.

Grandma didn't follow. She frowned at the clientele and left before midnight with Eliot and Teresa. Leah and I stayed to kill the second carafe of wine with the band.

Bleecker Street hadn't gone away. Leah carried my guitar in her right hand and held my right hand in her left; I carried the amp in my left, held Leah's left hand in my right. When we reached the car Leah stared at me across the roof. "Now may I tell you?"

I lowered the top and Leah was lost for a moment in a blur of collapsing vinyl. "All right."

She opened the door and got in. I stood paralyzed with expectation. She said, "You will have a nation of fans."

"I was good?"

"You made it look easy."

I sat beside her and stared at the dash. "A nation of fans!"

She put her arm around my shoulder. "The guitar and amp are still in the street, Tramp."

I stowed the amp in the trunk and propped the guitar in the backseat. I stared through the windshield. "A nation of fans!"

"Who will knock at your door to touch you."

I turned to her. "You will tell them I'm not in."

"No. I will be writing a book on speciesism—probably in Spain. You've gone for my bait, chump. You're guilty of an obvious thing—unredeeming self-absorption."

I lowered my head to the wheel and closed my eyes. Leah put her hand on the back of my neck, beneath my hair. I said, "We will become two swinging singles whose careers are more important than ourselves."

She pulled on my ear. "Don't get worked up now. Drive."

I put the key in the ignition. "We will be respective literary and musical stars who will sleep with everyone we want, be loaded, get loaded, make scandal magazines, take drugs, fly here, yacht there, die early—"

"Shush!"

I sighed and turned my head to her. "You be the ambulance driver and I'll be the patient."

We switched seats. Pulling out, Leah said, "Dearest, I'll do it tonight, but my house mustn't become your hospital, nor I your nurse."

"Put on the siren, Ms. Nightingale."

III

RED TRUCKS HAULED AWAY THE WRECKAGE OF THE LAST RE-
sort for a week. The road and the leaves of the trees bounding
the road were powdered with white dust. Merrill Miller and his
gang didn't miss their opportunity to hide behind sections of
broken walls and heave rocks and cement at one another.

By mid-August the lot was a square of hard flat mud used
by seashore vacationers for parking. A sign facing the Atlantic
announced:

COMING SOON
MODERN CONDOMINIUM ELEGANCE
CONSULT CENTURY REALTORS

Well, we are legged creatures and the world is a leg trap. I
waited and waited for Owen Chance to call, but he didn't.
When I finally phoned him his machine allowed that "Owen
Chance knows a place where dreams are born and time is never
planned. He has gone there for his twenty-ninth birthday."

At the tone I said, "Owen, my guy is losing his mind!" and
retired for four straight days to the beach with an overflowing

thermos of iced oolong tea, lemon slices and vodka. Leah had gone to Manhattan to observe an attempt to reintroduce peregrine falcons to an island whose pigeon population was in need of predation. She was staying at the apartment of her editor, a woman, undoubtedly lesbian, dedicated to destroying me by driving Leah across an ocean to complete a book on cruelty.

The ocean rolled in and rolled in and rolled in. I sat before this monotony Tuesday, Wednesday, Thursday and Friday, equipped daily with radio, the town newspaper and three Camel cigarettes laced with enough marijuana to hold my mind in a state of abeyance. On Thursday, I believe, I read an item of unusual local interest.

Pee Wee Regatta Victor Thanks Former Resort Owner

Seven-year-old Merrill Miller, skippering the battleship *Omaha* for vacationing Whitney Bottoms, the five-time Pee Wee champion, won the sixth annual Pee Wee radio-controlled craft regatta today with a record time of 30:08:13. Miller, a second-grader at Spring Lake Private School, finished two minutes ahead of James Tunnel, a police officer for the city of Avon-by-the Sea.

Miller lives with his mother and stepfather at 75 4th Avenue. Whitney Bottoms resides at 30 3rd Avenue with his wife, mother and daughter. His son, Waldo, was killed in a car accident last year.

James Tunnel finished second for the sixth straight year.

I closed my eyes, rolled onto my back and pretended this was the best of all possible worlds.

Family Disappointment Stuns Recording Industry with Smash LP!

Mr. Aldo Huxley Bottoms, known to the recording world as Tramp Bottoms, shocked skeptical family and friends today when it was announced that his first LP, *Very Tramp*, had reached number one on the nationwide survey of weekly record sales.

Someone touched my shoulder and I opened my eyes. Grandma stood above me with her friend, Sadie Fischgrund, at her side. "What's Sonny smiling so wide about?"

"Delusions of grandeur."

"Well, I got to ask sweetie to stick Grandma's umbrella in the sand."

I looked at them, at Sadie Fischgrund and Grandma, and I could hear time ticking away in their eyes.

Upon instruction, I set the umbrella down by the water, where the breeze is coolest, the sand the wettest. Once they were seated, Grandma said, "A man who don't sound like one called and said to call him right away."

"Owen Chance?"

"I wrote it down on the note pad by the telephone." Grandma was rummaging distractedly through her beach bag. "I brought Sonny a nice lunch, since he's getting so skinny."

My breath came back and I started to run. Grandma cried, "Sweetie forgot his lunch!" and I raced back to snatch it.

The message: SONNY CALL IRWIN.

Dialing the phone, I sank to my knees and lit a cigarette. The tape machine intoned: "God is music. Music is Tramp. Tramp is God." There was a click and then the voice of my manager came on the live wire.

"Owen!"

"Ah, king of pop 'n' roll!"

"What's cooking?"

"News, guy. Super manager has news."

With my heart slamming I lowered my head to the floor and closed my eyes. Despite my throat's contraction, I managed, "Shoot!"

Owen said, "Your manager has just returned to town and he has just heard from Jewel Daye. He wants us in the studio next week. We get three days to cut four numbers. Then he takes them to the top for a listen."

I raised my head and opened my eyes. "Say that again, Owen."

After he had, I said, "I can't breathe."

"Just let the minstrel gigolo be forewarned: This last step is the trickiest. We are still working in the Twilight Zone and the higher we go, the further we are entitled to fall."

"I hit bottom a long time ago, Owen."

"I'll meet you in Utopic's studios Monday. We'll speak before then. Regrettably, I have company at the moment."

"Owen!"

"Company that has begun to remove their clothing."

"Listen a minute."

"Hit it, guy."

"No one's ever helped me before. I want to thank you."

Just before the receiver hit the cradle, I heard Owen say, "If Torrey were to see what you're doing into that glass platter . . ."

I LOST PERSPECTIVE. WHAT I WANTED MORE THAN ANYTHING was to tell them: I haven't been a fool, they want me in the studio on Monday!

I ran for Leah. Lumber Lee and his son were finishing the deck in back. I shouted, "Where's Leah?" but by the time their hammering ceased, I remembered that Leah was in New York. I sat down in the driveway. I thought, run to New York City. Realizing, however, that the city was over an hour away by car, I dashed inside to tell Eliot; no one home. Then I ran back to the beach. Grandma and Mrs. Fischgrund were gone, probably for a goddamn walk. I raced home. A son should call his mother to share his lifetime's first little success.

No one answered in California. The Beach House School's number provided one busy signal after the other.

You fool, I thought, tell Dennis! Tell the little Airedale. I searched the family house, Leah's house, the park, Dennis' favorite jetties. I called the police. The sergeant said to try Mahoney, the humane officer. I called the number. No answer. I was addled and frightened.

Fifty states and the District of Columbia gas twenty-five million dogs and cats every year. Lives were on the line.

THE DOOR WAS LOCKED, THE LIGHTS EXTINGUISHED. I SEMICIR-cled the animal shelter and peeked in a rear window, cutting the glare with my hands.

I do not believe in much. At best, happiness is the temporary absence of pain. Pain always wants to come into your life. Pain is a rapist. My eyes scanned the cages. I worried that if I didn't find Dennis by sundown, I'd gas myself.

Then I saw him, saw Dennis, my son, in a cage. He was sitting there, lordly as a lion. I knocked and waved. He saw me but deigned not to respond. From his eyes, however, I could see that he was furious. The little Airedale was chewing on the bars in the adjacent cage.

The police station is next door. I crossed the parking lot to demand an immediate release. By coincidence, an Avanti was parked in this lot. A sticker—IMPOUNDED—was plastered across the windshield.

The officer at the desk was ordering a freely delivered veal parmigiana submarine, his back to me. Veal, of course, calls for a creature less than three months old.

"My dogs are in the pound and my car's been impounded. What gives!"

Lincoln Tunnel swiveled around in his chair. His smile, like Hitler's, warned of a bad odor and hinted at necrophilic tendencies. He referred to a stack of papers. "You've accumulated more than sixty dollars in tickets on an *unregistered* vehicle. Add that to a twenty-five-dollar tow charge, a fifty-dollar contempt-of-court fine, and it means she's yours for one hundred and thirty American dollars. As for the incarceration of the mutts, you got twenty-five per head for failure to register, plus ten dollars per collection charge. The male, it was pumping a poodle in plain view of children. The other pulled down a laundry line at the Hardys' place. You'll hear from their lawyer." He toted it up on the bill. "Two hundred dollars by certified check or money order to the Township of Avon or we'll be forced to dispose of confiscated merchandise properly."

"Merchandise!"

"I won't listen to abuse."

"Where's the humane officer?"

"Mahoney? He's gone, will be for the entire weekend. Them dogs won't starve. You come by Monday with your certified check or money order, and we'll see."

I took my leave. Statistically, my life is one-third finished, and by now I know better than to debate the intractably sadistic.

"I did what I did to you, Bottoms," Tunnel shouted, "to protect the decent sector of our community from your type of scum element."

A brook bounded by high cement walls runs between the rear of the shelter and the town's depot. When the train pulled in, I waved to the conductor; he waved back and blew the horn. I smashed the shelter's window with a rock the specific gravity of Lincoln Tunnel's cruelty.

I cleared away the sharp edges and dropped in head first. Then I crawled into the cage next to Dennis' and looked at him through the metal wires. "Dennis," I whispered, "guess what? Utopic Records has invited me to their studio to record four songs for executive review!"

Dennis has always believed in me, always loved and supported me. He wagged his tail and began to whine. When he came out of the cage and into my arms, I surprised myself by crying.

Lucy, on the other hand, backed away in fear when I opened the cage. I spoke her name and the puppy went epileptic with relief.

On the way out, I investigated the windowless room where the township committed what the Bible says is a shall-not. Two vents were visible in the ceiling; it was nothing less than a gas chamber.

I looked back at Lucy and Dennis. Then I dropped the terriers out the window one at a time before sneaking through myself. Thereafter, we escaped the world's cruel designs as fast as we could.

AT HOME GRANDMA WAS MUSING ON THE PORCH. I CAME UP THE stairs queerly on an imaginary pogo stick. Grandma said, "sssHHH!"

"Grandma! Guess what!"

"Shush!"

"What?" I said softly. "What's the matter?"

She leaned forward in her rocker. "I had my beet borsch all made and thought I'd go tidy up a bit. It ain't right to go into a room without knocking first, but there ain't been anyone in the guest room since Teresie's Scotty used to be alive." Grandma cleared her throat and her eyes held closed. "I opened the door with my pail and mop and raised the shades a peek, and there they was, fast asleep together without a stitch between them!" Grandma blushed. "I creeped out and closed the door. Now I'm writing to the President to see what he thinks."

"The President doesn't think, Grandma."

The old woman shook her head. "Grandpa and me didn't sleep together for three years. He was bashful and I was too. It ain't nice to do it too soon, Sonny."

I looked into the afternoon sky, where the moon floated in three-quarter luminescence. I had a point to make. "Listen, Grandma, my generation was raised on milk tainted with radio-active strontium 90 from aboveground nuclear testing. Also toxic waste polluted our processed baby food. We all fear bone cancer, an abbreviated life. Chemotherapy is always on the horizon. Sex, on the other hand, is intelligible. It can be performed in the safety of one's own bed. See what I mean?"

Grandma watched Lucy and Dennis sniffing something on the lawn. "You don't see children feeding birds no more, sweetie, so much as walking around with radios in their ears. There ain't ten people who know how to can or pickle. No, people don't know how to live no more. It's like they forgot what is and ain't good for themselves." Grandma met my eyes. "It's like the earth ain't my home no more."

Around then the tremolos began. At first I thought it was the trilling of a dove or robin. In fact, it was Teresa's sighs.

Grandma was curious. "What's that?"

I cried "Me!" and began howling at the terriers. Lucy charged up the steps and barked incessantly at me like a man's best friend.

Sometime later Teresa and Eliot appeared on the porch. After a silence in which we each stared abashedly at the terriers, Grandma said guilefully, "Was you two inside all this time? We didn't even know. We been at the park feeding the ducks till just now. Right, Sonny?"

"That's right." I nodded nervously. "Fucking ducks."

IV

SATURDAY MORNING'S MAIL BROUGHT A POSTCARD ALL THE way from Campeche, Mexico.

Dear Son and Daughter:
    Daddy's room is white. There is a bed and there is a desk, and they both overlook the Bay of Campeche. I eat fish; I eat fruit. I am the only tourist in the place, and it is hotter than hell.
    I have nothing now but I am the happiest man alive. What it was was boredom and guilt: the two great human poisons.
    I have the first chapter of my novel, *Peace and War,* completed. I've wasted the better part of my life to date and this book tries to explain why.
    Please write to your father in obeisance to the commandment regarding Honor.

Love,
Dad

A second correspondence, typed on yellow paper in capital letters to resemble a telegram, read:

BOY WONDER! STOP HOME FROM NYC STOP THE GIRL OF YOUR DREAMS

There was a plumber's truck in front of her house and an electrician's truck as well. Leah was wearing a little madras dress reminiscent of our collegiate past. As I studied her it occurred to me that since this century's commencement, more than fifty million people have died in wars staged to quench one or another empire's thirst for natural resources. All these freshly dead lay silently beneath us in the earth. The earth, therefore, is full of bones. Of cow bones, sheep bones, chicken bones, the bones of the "racially impure," the bones of soldiers, of horses, Indians, the bones of terrified children. The earth is a cemetery. It is upon this earth, I thought, that I am trying to express my love for Leah Summit.

Leah was in a state. I could see it in her eyes when I kissed her hello.

"Eliot and I botched the wiring job and the maple tree's roots have blocked the main sewer line, which is damn expensive and time-consuming. I've got a deadline on a book. I'm not working enough. I've *got* to get away from here!" She began to twirl in circles on the sidewalk, simultaneously issuing a noise resembling a siren.

I stopped her spinning and led her through the collapsing gate into the yard. Concentrating, I declaimed, "I finally understand that we are too far down the road of mankind's historical madness to be anything but eternally grateful for the smallest physical space and most tenuous emotional opportunity to live together and try to love each other."

"I've got to get this book done; I'm over my head. I can't afford to be sentimental."

"Aw, Leah." Then, noting her distraction, I said again, "Leah?"

She blinked at me. I held up my right hand. "How many fingers?"

"You can live in the house, Tramp. I'll be gone less than a

year. When I return you'll be mature, with the monkey of success off your back. So will I. We'll know better then."

"Earth to Summit, over."

Her eyes cleared. "When did you get here?"

"Just did. You know what?"

"What?"

"Utopic Records wants me in their recording studio on Monday!"

Leah's eyes opened wide as I've ever seen them open.

"You're the only one who knows—except Dennis."

"Oh, Tramp!" She grabbed my nose.

"It's just a demo session." I sounded like an operator. "Could be a case of close-but-no-cigar."

She hugged me to her. "I really will be back before you know it."

I put my head on her shoulder.

She said, "We were innocent once. You ruined it."

"If I win the Ocean County Marathon, will you stay?"

"If you win."

"What if I just finish?"

"You must win."

She held me at arm's length and scrutinized me: I cannot say I blame a woman for being skeptical of a man's sincerity.

"If you stay," I promised, "I'll paint your house, buy you flowers every day, never get nasty, stop being thoughtless . . ."

Leah smiled ambiguously and walked away. I watched her enter the house.

"Be mature," I cried, "do everything your way, always be supportive, *apologize to your mother!*"

Leah looked out her window. "You still there?"

I went to the window. "Type your manuscript, do the dishes, consult a psychiatrist—"

The electrician called out behind her, "Where's the fuse box, honey?"

Leah said, "Honey?" Then she turned to me. "Here's your big chance."

I hurried indoors. "Don't call the lady honey, buster. Her name is Ms. Summit. Mine's Tramp."

I turned to Leah for approval. She winked.

"About the fuse box," the electrician said.

"Ms. Summit is very busy at the moment. Follow me, please." I located the control panel in the basement with such ease and facility that someone might have thought the place was partly mine.

ON SUNDAY I PLACED THE FOLLOWING LETTER IN LEAH'S MAIL box.

Dear Leah,

As we both know from experience, Tramp is a neurasthenic with self-pitying and self-destructive tendencies. Frankly, I am concerned that he might not survive your going away. For his sake as well as mine, I hope you will consider staying with him. Sincerely yours,

Your stepdog
Dennis

Monday morning I wheeled Teresa to work. The ocean breeze was stiff and lashed my sister's bronze-colored hair this way and that. She was wearing a pink cotton dress, a gift from Eliot Howard.

"I want to talk with you about something." She reclined her head against the back of the wheelchair and stared straight up into my eyes. Her long eyelashes were sorrel in the sunlight.

"Talk-ho," I said.

"Tell me what you think of Eliot."

"I think what matters is what you think of him."

The sun was a cool, white August sun; Teresa closed her eyes and faced its diminishing warmth.

"He's a very tender person," she said. "His former wife has hurt him very deeply, but he doesn't seem capable of bitterness. He's remarkably kind and wants to lead a simple life. I can't think of anything I dislike about him, except that I'm lonely when he's not with me."

When she opened her eyes, I said, "Sounds as if you've found your man, Missus Bottoms."

I straightened up after kissing her forehead and discovered we'd reached the school: a white building on a treeless lawn directly across the avenue from the Atlantic. The building was encircled by beds of red geraniums.

"Yesterday," my sister said, "he proposed we rent a little apartment together."

The front door opened and a group of adults with strange eyes came down the walkway, followed by a young woman. A man with a Neanderthal forehead and thick-lensed eyeglasses walked directly to Teresa. "You my teaker doo! You teak me do read. Dis udder teaker teak uz do buy vood an' ride da buz." The man turned to me and smiled. "My name Genny. Dese my new pandz. I god dem uzed. I gan read and cound do zeven. Wand do hear me? One, do, dree, vor, vive, zix, zeven!" He shook my hand and the group loaded into a school van.

I turned to Teresa. "Wah'd you dell Eliod?"

"That I'd think about it. What do you think?"

"I think," I said, "that you deserve to be happy more than anyone I know."

She looked into her lap and then into my eyes. A bell rang inside the building; Teresa consulted her wristwatch. "I'll be late. We'll talk more later."

She wheeled herself to the front-door ramp before she turned. Her hair blew across her face in a gust of wind and she hooked it behind her ears.

A motorcycle thundered past.

I blew her a kiss good-bye.

ELIOT WAS INSTALLING A PICTURE WINDOW IN LEAH'S BED-
room. Leah was lying on her bed—a mattress on a box spring,
no frame—and staring at the ceiling, the phone at her ear.
"You promised me those tiles a month ago. Now you deliver
pink ones!" She held one above her head and examined it. "I
ordered beige. Beige is not pink." She listened. "My workmen
can't wait a *month* for beige tiles. My workmen are in my
house now!" She listened again. "Tough? What do you mean,
tough!"

If we were married, Leah and I, she might say, might be
inclined to threaten, "Wait until my husband hears about
this!" When she hung up she groaned "Spain!" and lay her arm
over her eyes. The phone rang again. She said wearily, "Someone get that, please."

I picked up the receiver. "And another thing!" I began.

"Hellew, Eliot?"

"Grandma!"

"This is Sonny's grandma. Eliot?"

"He's installing a picture window, Grandma."

"Who's this? Eliot?"

"It's Sonny, Grandma. Sonny."

"Sonny? Hold on, I'll get him."

"Grandma!"

I heard the phone drop. I told Eliot that Grandma wanted
to speak with him and ran home.

When I arrived Grandma was calling me from the porch.
Dennis, imitating a sphinx, sat rigid as rock. I bounded up the
steps.

"That's right, Sonny. Hurry! Eliot's waiting on the phone."

I picked up the receiver in the living room.

"Hello? Hello?"

"Eliot!"

"Tramp?"

"Hi."

"What is this?"

"Respect for the aged."

"What?"

"Just hold on. Grandma," I called, "Eliot's on the phone now."

She smiled. "All right, Sonny, thanks." She put the plastic to her wrinkled face. "Hellew?" Then she told Eliot that Teresa expected him for dinner at seven, and hung up.

"What about Leah?" I asked.

Grandma blinked. "Leah?"

"Leah Summit."

"Who?"

"Leah Summit. My girl friend."

"Oohh, Leah! I got to call her next. What's her number, Sonny?"

WE HAD DINNER IN THE KITCHEN. GRANDMA AND LEAH SERVED the food. I poured the wine. Thrice I squeezed Leah's hand under the table and she squeezed back every time. After that I hit the bottle wildly. At one point Grandma said, "Where Leah is used to be Grandpa. Teresa was Mommy and Eliot was my son, Whit." When she turned to me she said, "You was the baby, Uncle Spud. He was so skinny we had to stuff him with potatoes and cream." She bowed her head. "Someday Leah will be me, or Teresa will. Once I was just like them." She shook her head at this mystery. "Ain't life beautiful, children. So fast but so beautiful!"

I smiled. If I'd spoken my mind: *Not particularly.*

After coffee and Grandma's incomparable devil's food cake, we all got smashed on cognac and played twenty questions on the porch. No one guessed Erik Satie, Enos Slaughter, Sun Yat-Sen, Kate Chopin, Edmundo Desnoes. I chanced to think that one day I might make somebody's list.

We strolled to the boardwalk in the dark and watched the stars over the Atlantic. Grandma said, "Soon the house won't be ours no more. It ain't right not to fill it once more and be happy."

Everyone, therefore, stayed the night. Teresa and I and Grandma in our respective rooms, Leah in the guest room, Eliot on a cot in what was once my room. Naturally, after the lights went out, there were adjustments. Eliot and I, for example, bumped into each other in the darkened hallway.

In the morning I crawled from bed without disturbing Leah and ran on the beach beneath the sun's warming ascension. When I returned Eliot and Teresa and Leah were sipping coffee on the porch. Grandma was standing in the vegetable garden in her bathrobe, talking to the tomatoes.

Home.

Driving to the Utopic recording studio later that morning, I acknowledged that my music was primarily a means of reacquiring what I had just left. At the same time, after spending three days in a sound studio recording four songs, I understood that, as with Dorothy, it would take far more than a fraudulent wizard to reappropriate my lost sense of shelter.

V

I HAD NEVER RUN TWENTY-SIX MILES AND THREE HUNDRED ODD yards. The farthest I'd ever run, excluding the distances accumulated in twenty-five years of flight, was fifteen miles. I had never run a formal race, neither a six- nor a ten-miler. I had never experienced God while running, never achieved at-onement with nature while running, never reached orgasm.

I didn't really train for the race. I didn't work out with a beer-drinking buddy or arrange for people to administer water to me along the route. My plan was simply to run faster than anyone else.

The race was designed to begin in Long Branch and continue down the coast on Ocean Drive to Spring Lake, where it would turn inland and where, I envisioned, I would break quickly and follow the official road-club truck to the finish line. In victory I would win eternal life for Grandma, Leah's permanent presence by my side, harmony between my parents, a pair of robust legs for my sister, the resurrection of my grandfather, a lifetime box of dog biscuits for Dennis, a record contract for myself.

Naturally, a runner does not desire sun and heat. Neverthe-
less, all three thousand of us got it: cloudless and eighty-seven
degrees at ten in the morning. I wore white shorts and a blue
T-shirt with LAST RESORT printed in white letters on the front.
My hair was in a braid with a blue bandanna around my
forehead. My number was 2789. Around my neck, tied with
sewing thread, hung the little rubber cow.

There were helicopters overhead to spot us and a motorcycle
entourage to keep spectators back. A small circle of acquain-
tances was informed to look for me leading the way at the
ten-mile marker at Bradley Beach. In the end, I thought, when
I win, they will applaud and applaud, a reporter will take my
photograph, I will say to those who have not believed in me,
not respected me: There—you see!

At the gun I was touching my toes, stretching my ham-
strings. The trick, they say, is to start quickly, run like hell for
a mile or two, then settle into a pace, keep your head from
dropping, hold your back straight and your arms down.

I ran hard for the first two miles. The headline: FAMILY JOKE
LAUGHS LAST! At five miles someone called, "One hundred!"
and pointed at me. I thought, pick it up, kid, pick it up, Tramp
baby, and ran on through the heat, sweat dripping off me and
stinging my eyes.

If you're lucky, what sets in is a trance; the mind dissolves
and the body functions mechanically. Automatic pilot. This
happened for a time. Somewhere, however, around the seventh
mile my brain requested information from my heart as to what
the hell I was doing. Redeeming a past reputation, I thought,
and pressed on, forcing upon myself a pace I'd never before
maintained.

People were holding out cups of water at the eight-mile turn.
I passed six runners who had stopped to drink and decided to
drink at the finish line, drink in the winner's circle, drink before

the cameras. My braid came apart at my accelerated pace and my hair flew out and away like Chief Joseph's or Lauren Hutton's.

I swished on.

At nine miles people tended to refer to their watches. Around this time I realized my left ankle felt broken and my sight was blurring. People were applauding. Someone screamed, "Two minutes from the leader!" and something in my heart, a stubbornness that has always been infuriating to others and preserving to myself, implored me to pick it up. I did.

I looked for them at ten miles. I can count, you see, maybe to four before the people of this world become nothing but a herd of repugnant strangers. I didn't see them. This hurt nearly as much as the ache that had begun in my ankle and spread up my leg. I was limping slightly, though still soaring along, when I became aware that my breathing had grown labored. Still, I struggled through Bradley Beach, refusing to slow my pace. Someone screamed, *"Do it, Chief,"* and held out water. I raced past, groaning.

Something went very wrong. I heard them scream "Yeah, Tramp!" and "Go, Aldo!" as if in a dream. I turned to wave but the spectators floated and blurred. Then my head seemed to be running by itself, my feet so weightless that I could not judge when they were striking the macadam. My ears buzzed and I could hear my heart pounding like it was about to explode. This, I thought, is the euphoria they speak of, I have broken *the wall;* I'm approaching God, else God is coming for me. Then the earth sailed away from me in a flash of darkness and I was flying through space.

I came to, supine on a mattress in a dirt field. A mask was clamped over my mouth and nose. "Breathe slowly and evenly, remain calm." A tube extended into my arm from a bottle that dangled from the hand of a woman in white. "You fainted from dehydration." She smiled.

I removed the mask and sat up. "I've never won anything in my life until today."

"Perhaps next year," she said, and the truth of my latest flop bowed my head.

I was fighting tears when they appeared at the side of the ambulance. I'd gone down in the nineteenth position, roughly ten miles and six hundred yards from the starting line, approximately ten feet from a vacant lot where, not long ago, a place called the Last Resort once stood.

Of the 3,000 contestants who entered the marathon, 2,569 finished. For better than ten miles I had run better than 2,549 of the loathsome bastards; this I let my family know emphatically.

"With all that gorgeous hair," Leah said, "you looked as brave as George Custer, going down like that."

I stood up and pulled off my bandanna and the stupid little cow. Leah had her arm around my waist.

"Let's face it," I said, "I'm a musician, not a goddamn Greek."

"Also," Leah said, "the only man I have ever loved."

VI

OWEN SAID TO GIVE THE UTOPIC EXECUTIVES AT LEAST A WEEK
after our last day of recording, and I did. I ran a race with
ungainly honor, exhibiting raw promise and brio, if not intelligence and discipline. But thereafter I was a simple wreck. I
avoided everyone; didn't shave, prayed to my amulets twice a
day; lay on my surfboard with my life flashing before me in the
sky; rode the Ferris wheel in Asbury Park every twilight, har-
boring superstitious beliefs; walked seven miles nightly to Deal
and about twelve back, humming my four recordings as persis-
tently as primitives chant incantations. Needless to say, I
couldn't eat or sleep, and by the tenth day of no word I had
rings under my eyes and a funereal opacity in my pupils.

One morning, walking home at dawn with a can of beer in
my hand, I discovered the following sign posted on the front
lawn of the house:

ANOTHER EXCLUSIVE PROPERTY

FOR SALE

BY

CENTURY REALTY

Well, I was already in an acute state of exhaustion and vulnerability. When I saw the sign before my home, the house where I was raised, where I knew every angle of vision from every window, where I had escaped from the world for so many years, the lawn where so many dead birds had been buried and eulogized—when I saw this sign I began to cry. I placed my forehead to the grass and let my sorrow flow.

When I lifted my head, I thought, what is there left for us? The empire is crumbling, evangelists are pouring from their sewers, toxic wastes work deformations upon the newborn and nuclear reentry vehicles encircle the earth's stratosphere. But what is left—and if not left, what must be regained—is what there has always been: one's house, one's dog, one's favorite shade tree, one's girl, the feel of her waist, that secret place beneath her hair just behind her earring. In a word, *home.*

True, our head is also a home; our head is where we live out our stupefied life. But a house is where we lay our heads to rest. And though we build our homes upon the earth, from the earth, the earth is not our home; the earth is our grave; we build homes to protect our heads from the earth.

I walked mournfully to the Atlantic and stared at the horizon, at the remorseless sun rising in the firmament. Gulls were scavenging the dead; and a woman possessing long black hair and wearing cutoffs and a blue sweat shirt sat near the shoreline.

I sat beside her. She remained staring at the water.

"Can't sleep," I said. "You?"

"Ditto."

"Thinking, thinking, thinking," I said.

"Ditto for me."

"That expression," I said, " 'Two heads are better than one.' Maybe we could help each other."

"Two hearts," she answered, "two minds, two wills. It's so hard to get all three synchronized."

"For a while there we did."

"We were young."

"I can't remember the last time I ate. You?" I lit Leah's cigarette, then my own. With the sun's increasing ascension a wind came from the ocean. The sun was round and white, but not warm.

Leah said, "Just listen a second," and smoke plumed from her nose.

I spoke bravely, "Don't even bother saying it. I'll water your plants when you're gone; I'll cry on them twice a day. I'll hang my regrets on your laundry line and make sure your pipes don't freeze like my heart. I'll sit on the porch, pretending you're inside typing away, and whistle a happy tune."

Leah extinguished her cigarette in the sand. "I'm sure you realize how much we, my editor and I, thought about it and how difficult it's going to be for me too." She looked away, down the beach. "I've got all the research finished, at last. What I need now is uninterrupted writing time."

"Spain," I said to the water. "Leah's going to Spain."

"I thought maybe you'd live in the house, take care of the puppy, water—"

"—the plants."

She looked straight at me. "All this emotional turmoil . . . I can't work in the middle of it. It's not the same as writing songs."

In my eyes the sun was now a long liquid flare on the horizon.

"Don't cry," Leah said.

I dashed my eyes with my hand. "I'm not."

She put her arm around me. "Weepy the music man."

I covered my eyes, but the tears leaked through my fingers.

"It's waiting to hear from the record people," she said. "Poor Mick Haggard." When I got control of myself, Leah said, "How about a skinny dip to wash away our sins?"

We took off each other's clothes.

I do not swim well. Leah, contrarily, is graceful as a porpoise. I followed her into deep water and quickly tired. She wouldn't let me return to the shallows.

"I'll drown," I laughed, and took in a mouthful. She pushed me under. When I began to cough and flail my arms, she came to my rescue.

Onshore she said, "I think it turns you on to be saved," and looked to my crotch for validation. When the water is cold it happens; it shrinks away to nothing. Leah gave me a hand and changed all that. Then we lay down on the wet sand. The slope of the beach was such that we were hidden from Ocean Avenue and the old white houses bounding the avenue.

For a change I was on top, Leah on the bottom. Then we rested side by side, facing each other, beneath a blanket. When I opened an eye, Leah was sleeping. I covered my face with her hair and attempted the same.

In three weeks it would be autumn.

THE REALTOR, A MIDDLE-AGED WOMAN WITH SILVER HAIR, came to the house that morning to assess our home's market value. Realtors are as polite as funeral directors, subtle as tapeworms.

Among other things, Grandma let it be known that her husband, Hodge, had purchased the house in 1925 for twenty thousand dollars and bequeathed it to her son, Whitney, in 1958. The furnace and plumbing were originals and still good as new. I, meanwhile, silently implored Grandma to dump upon this woman a load of contempt, but Grandma lacks the testosterone necessary for battle. The last thing she said was, "Older is always better, Mrs. Coleman, only if you ain't living."

That same day I spoke with my mother about the sale. I could tell she wasn't listening. She had decided to lease a high-fashion boutique in Sausalito with her sister and needed the house money to finance the business.

"I'm afraid I simply must sell the house, dear. I've discussed it with everyone here at the institute. It's a financial necessity, not to mention an essential psychological unburdening. You see, dear, by selling the house I liberate myself from the very structure of my past enslavement; without a house for children and in-laws, a family physically dissolves. My condominium here is small, without any guest facilities, though there are a number of conveniently located motels if you should ever decide to visit. Furthermore, dear, your father and I have decided that he shall be entitled to the money from the sale of the resort, and I shall claim, exclusively, all monies from the sale of the house and the insurance on my wonderful little shack which you burned to the ground. I know that you harbor a sentimental attachment to the house, Aldo, but you've been away for nearly seven years, during which time you rarely visited. You're no less selfish than anyone else, and you must never forget that."

"What about Grandma?"

"Who?"

"Grandma!"

"Oh! Well, dear, your grandmother does have her apartment in Florida. She'll just have to make arrangements with the subtenants."

I gazed out the window of the house, heart constricted with fear and trembling. "Grandma shouldn't be all alone, Mother."

"What matters most these days," my mother said adamantly, "is protecting ourselves from one another, one day at a time. Each of us, I'm afraid, is all alone by design."

I didn't say anything. Outside, the sycamore surrendered seven brown leaves to the wind.

"I do wish I could be more spontaneous and magnanimous, dear, but of late I've come to terms with such unspeakable pain and anguish that in order to survive I simply can no longer afford to. I'm ever so sorry—really, I am."

"Oh well," I said evenly, "good luck in your chosen field," and returned the receiver to its pink cradle.

I HAVE ALWAYS CLUNG TO THINGS FOR FEAR OF FALLING AWAY entirely. Bedclothes, pillows, Dennis, Leah. Following the conversation with my mother, I was holding the terrier closely, my ear to his mortal chest, when the phone rang. Given my mood, given the absence of an adjustment neurosis, the ringing invaded my attic asylum like a civil-defense alarm.

I have always wanted a place to hide and have never found one. When, as a kid, I hid under the bed on school days, they would poke me out with a broom.

Dennis sat up on the fourth ring, his ears aimed in different directions. This *registered*—that is, stopped time's swift passage so that if I live to be two hundred, if I am reincarnated three dozen times, I shall always remember Dennis' brown eyes and his ludicrous ears as they appeared at that particular moment.

On the seventh ring, thinking that perhaps Leah was phoning to announce her decision to abort the Spanish escapade, I shot toward the ringing just as it stopped.

Grandma was surmounting the stairway one step at a time, putting two hands on the banister and pulling herself up. She was breathless. "It's for you, Sonny."

The phone awaited at the base of the stairs. Meanwhile, there was something clearly wrong with Grandma, and her eyes couldn't hide it.

"I ain't sure what it is, sweetie. I got up this morning with something not right. My legs ain't working. You got to take lunch by yourself." She stood below me staring fearfully, her white hair, her face of wrinkles.

I helped her to her room, into her bed, and covered her legs with an afghan. I placed my hand gently on her forehead, closed my eyes and prayed: Dear God, take ten of my years and give them to Grandma. Then I ran down the stairs to the phone.

"This is Owen Chance, manager of rock stars with chips on their shoulders, phoning from Spring Street Studio."

"Finally!"

"I do apologize, guy, but I've been involved in a beyond-good-and-evil amour with the lead singer of a Latin dance band. She's twenty with twice that many tricks. Even so, the notion that Latin girls have an endemic chancre problem is unfair. That they're spitfires is another thing. When she came it was like a water bed breaking; I'd never felt any-thing like it. I had to turn her over to satisfy my need for squeeze."

"This is a party line, Owen."

"All right, guy. Truth is, I've learned something, but certainly not everything."

The living room was dark and empty. I sat down in the shadows of the stairwell. "Tell me."

"It's completely unofficial, guy, which means you must erase it from your brain as soon as you hear it."

"Tell me."

"This comes from Julian Daye's former assistant, Patty

Wyatt, who was fired from Utopic in their housecleaning. She and Torrey bump bottoms at the Ritz when they're in need of working-class thrills. Anyway, Patty told Torrey that Julian told her that one of Utopic's VPs thinks you are a real comer with lyric wizardry."

"Meaning what?"

"Meaning squat, guy. Squat. Albeit, according to Patty Wyatt, the VP thinks you are a natural balladeer who has captured the ache of the age. Rumor has it that if the VP can convince the executive committee to come *hep me now,* that he'll purchase the recording rights to a Tramp Bottoms song or two."

"Translate, Owen."

"Potential megabucks, guy. A start. Though, obviously, without a contract with dry ink it means zero. With a contract, however, then the gigolo might be listening none-too-soon to one of guy's super tunes shooting to the top."

"You mean I might be a songwriter?"

"Right on, guy. A classy songster à la Mitchell, Prine, Browne and Taylor in their beginnings."

I stared through the living room window, pipe-dreaming.

"I shouldn't tell guy this, but super manager thinks guy is on his way to Oz. As for when we'll know, Mr. Chance cannot tell his guy this yet. I've put in calls to both Kid Johnnie and J. Daye, but both are at a record fair in LA. We could hear tomorrow, we could hear six weeks hence. What my virtuoso must do, meanwhile, is expand his ouevre with more and more Tramp smashes while keeping his head out of the clouds and other dark places. Be assured that Owen will phone as soon he hears more. Just remember, guy, the worst thing in life next to unknown rocker/writer is the life of the unknown rocker/writer's manager. Adieu to you."

I RAN TO LEAH'S HOUSE. WHEN I STEPPED INDOORS, ELIOT Howard and Lumber Lee Fields, both wearing painter's hats and pants, stood on two different ladders while smashing a hole in the ceiling. Lumber's son, Jack Fields, wheeled a barrowful of bricks through the front door. I surmised fireplace.

"She's gone to buy a suitcase and duffel bag," Eliot said, and a large section of ceiling fell six feet to my head. I stood covered with white plasterboard dust. Eliot looked on. "Has Teresa spoken with you lately?"

I dusted off. "Regarding what?"

"Our decision to live together."

Lumber Lee halted work and stared down at me, a cigarette hanging from his mouth; he was squinting to keep the smoke from his eyes. "We got work," he told Eliot. Then he said to me, "Whyn't you join our work force rather'n talking at it? Jack, for instance, needs unloading help with his freight."

"Say please, please."

"Shit."

Carrying in the next barrowful of bricks, I thought, I am helping Leah build a home and I am not frightened. Maybe after years of tearing things down you can begin to build them back up. I addressed young Fields. "A home isn't someplace you build in order to hide from the world, but to better enjoy it, right?"

Jack glanced furtively at his father, above us on the ladder. "My dad," he said nervously, "don't like his work force talking till lunch break."

Unloading the bricks, I said, "Maybe I dream about destruction too much. Does it make you happy to build things like chimneys and walls?"

Lumber Lee growled through his wreckage. "I hear my work force talking!"

"The Lord's the only thing ever made me feel right," Jack whispered.

Well, Jack, Jesus and I, all three, drove to Neptune City for a truckload of bricks. When we returned Lumber Lee and Eliot Howard were eating lunch on the front porch. Lumber bit into a whole Bermuda onion, working toward Nixonian breath.

"Here's my boys working on their lunchtime, and only got ten minutes left!" He winked at Eliot. "In your interim," he said to me, "your missus been here and gone to the travel-agency people in Belmar. I told her you broke down and worked for once."

I didn't say anything, merely booted the onion cleanly from the big mouth's hand. It sailed over the fence and rolled under Eliot's Fiat.

Lumber called after me, "Up your heine! I got three more in my lunch pail!"

THE HOUSE SOLD ON THE LAST FRIDAY OF AUGUST, THE DAY before Labor Day weekend. I didn't inquire into the details for the same reason I do not stare into caskets or public toilet bowls. The realty woman, Mrs. Coleman, drove a four-door silver-colored Cadillac to match her hair, and this left me wondering if her most private holes might not be filled with nickels and dimes. Mrs. Havermoore, the new owner, wore her blond hair tied fastidiously in a bun above her thin, immaculate face. The second time I saw her, the time she brought Mr. Havermoore along for his approval, she was wearing a yellow golfing skirt and shirt, and her husband was dressed in yellow tennis clothes with two yellow sweatbands around his wrists. He was drinking a bottle of Squirt. With them was a second woman—very thin, diseasedly thin, with mannish hair—who chain-smoked. This was the Havermoores' interior designer—

as distinguished, Mrs. Havermoore told Grandma, from their interior decorator.

There's a good deal one can say about the very wealthy. For the most part it has been said before. I should like to emphasize, however, that the trouble with the wealthy, the reason so many of us dislike them, results from the incommensurate relationship between their intelligence and their power, the latter being so undeservedly greater.

Naturally, my mother approved of the sale. The closing date was scheduled far enough into the fall to allow Grandma sufficient time to repossess her Florida apartment, which she had decided against returning to after my grandfather's extinction the previous summer.

I would have thought the very old—living as they do so near the final breath, the final heartbeat, final word, meal, smile, blink of the eye; sensing the darkness, sensing the smallness of their final resting or the roar of the crematorium flames— would not be as troubled by loss, loss in general, as the very young or the younger, the ones farther back in line from the end. But it seems to trouble them more. Take away an old lady's favorite chair, the view from her favorite sunny window, her flower box, break her toaster or favorite sugar-and-cream tray—do this, and you break her fragile claim on a diminishing world.

My particular grandmother responded to the sale of the house by walking to the beach each morning and sitting by herself at shoreline under a large yellow hat. She sat alone and watched the waves; occasionally she read a book.

There is order in waves: They come in and come in and come in. When there is nothing else, when everything else has crumbled beneath you, there are always the waves.

VII

THE DAY AFTER THE HOUSE WAS SOLD, GRANDMA RECEIVED A letter from my father. I have a tendency to disregard to whom epistles are addressed. It was right there on the kitchen table; had already been opened. I'd never seen such a long letter. I mostly read the parts pertaining to me.

I always felt I was a good son to you and Pop but as a father I didn't seem to have the stuff. Maybe it wasn't all my fault. You and Pop were happy together and you made me and Spud want families of our own. That's where you and Pop succeeded. Personally, I was never happy with Vera. It was the mistake of my life and I knew it early on, but after the twins there was nothing I could think of to do about it. That's where I failed as a father—in not loving my wife.

I loved my twins, though—the boy and little girl. Somehow after they went away to school I never got them back. The boy more so than the girl. At least she'd come to visit from the city on weekends with her boyfriend, but my boy never seemed happy in the house after he left it for school. I can't say I don't understand it. Two people, like his mother and me, who don't get along put out a poison that's obvious to other people. Aldo always hurt easily to begin with. Further, he was attached to me in a strange and strong way, and I knew sooner or later I'd disappoint him. He never had too many friends, always a dog and his sister, and later on Leah Summit. He was a loner by nature. I bought him Jocko hoping a dog would make him more secure. Of course, after that time Jocko got run over and killed it seemed to do more harm that it was worth. He always cried a lot after that, almost over anything. What he found after Jocko was his music. That and Dennis, who his sister bought him for Christmas.

Aldo was smart, but never liked school. Just his rock band and his guitar. Then Leah. All in all I never understood him well enough to help him. I did try. If he hates me now he's wrong to, but maybe you could remind him of how hard I tried before I fell apart myself from unhappiness.

His mother and I always hoped that he and Leah would work things out. Without her he didn't seem to know how to tie his shoelaces. What happened to end things between them I have no idea. I stopped talking seriously to Aldo years ago because I was always afraid of saying the wrong thing to him. Then when things collapsed between Vera and me, and then the car accident when we thought we might lose our girl—after that I admit I stopped trying or really caring. It got to be too much.

I was always good with children. I still am, though after twelve they tend to grow disenchanted with me. I've been thinking lately that the reason parents always want their children to have children is in the hope that their children's parenthood will help them understand their own parents and eventually forgive them for any unintentional errors they may have made.

You know, my life hasn't amounted to very much. I wanted to be a writer and never got started. Maybe it ruined my life and maybe it didn't, but I know I've been scared all along for Aldo that musical dreams would ruin his. Somehow if a man's daughter doesn't respond to him it's bearable, but when a man's son doesn't love him it not only hurts to the bone, but angers—maybe because a man's son can remind him of how the man felt about his own father. I guess what matters, though, is how we live without ever knowing much about anyone else.

All I want now is peace. I don't like living alone; I don't like when on the other side of the newspaper there's only an empty chair. Vera has rented me a place near her sister's in Sausalito. We spoke last night, but I don't know what's going to happen. Maybe I need her as an excuse for why I'm unhappy. She says she looks ten years younger from lack of aggravation and that my apartment overlooks the bay and is an ideal place for a writer. It sounds like Brooklyn thirty years ago, with me planning to write and Vera working; but maybe this time it will work.

I'm fifty-nine now. I'm old enough to know that a person's world is as small as his family, and himself only as large as his family. Maybe life amounts to no more than trying to learn something about those who created you and those you created.

I folded the letter and stuffed it into its envelope.

TERESA WAS EMPLOYED FULL-TIME, GRANDMA WAS TOO OLD, my mother and father were at least three thousand miles away: To wit, it was incumbent on me to begin packing up the house —stacking what furniture was left, emptying the closets, boxing the rest. I was in the attic doing just this—folding curtains and roping together stacks of books—when Leah came clambering up the stairs in a pair of clogs and a loose white dress. Her hair, freshly washed, had auburn sunstreaks.

"Well," she said, catching her breath, "I'm all ready to go."

I nodded and resumed roping.

"The house is nearly finished. You can live in it for free if you like."

"Never!"

"You can put your Wurlitzer in the living room by the new picture window. You'll have Dennis for company, Lucy if you like."

"Also your ghost."

"I told Teresa and Eliot that they could have the place if you didn't want it. Should I tell them yes?"

"I can't picture sitting by myself in front of your fireplace knowing full well that you're screwing some matador with silk pants."

"I'd think he'd take them off first, don't you?"

I stared at my feet. "I wouldn't have played the piano or guitar while you were working. I'd have cooked all the meals and raked leaves, shoveled snow and cut firewood. You would've knocked off that book in no time."

"Please," Leah said, "don't."

"Bought you a ring, let your mother throw the wedding, changed my name to Mr. Summit. I'd have beat up people who whistled at you, typed up your manuscripts, carried your books home from the library, answered the phone when you were writing, mopped the floors, vacuumed the rugs, cleaned the gutters, emptied the garbage, done the dishes."

"Tramp?"

"It would have been different than it was lately. I'm almost a songwriter; Utopic is on the verge. I'm almost a man now."

"And maybe," Leah said, "we are just a habit we should learn to break?"

I looked at her and smiled bravely. "Listen, Leah, have a great time in Spain. Go to museums, get lots of writing done, entertain the Spanish soccer team, the Davis Cup tennis team, go for joy rides with Falangists, meet Mediterranean lesbians, swim naked through the Pillars of Hercules, tan your buns on the Rock of Gibraltar, see Seville, visit Valencia, fuck Franco."

"Franco's dead, Tramp."

"It's been done."

She closed her eyes. "I'm leaving Tuesday. Make up your crazy mind within the next day or two about the house."

She started down the stairs.

From the landing I called, "You never loved me! You only wanted to marry me!"

She turned. "I used you for your body for seven years. Now

that every cell in both of us has changed, there's just no point."

"Someone should teach you what's funny!"

"An intro course in the meaning of constructive partnership wouldn't do you any harm!" She turned and started away.

I ran down two flights of stairs to watch her go out the front door. "Bye-bye. So long, rots a ruck, nice knowing you. Life's just a war against disappearances, beginning with the tooth fairy!"

Leah descended the porch steps as abruptly as if she'd fallen off the edge of the world.

LABOR DAY MONDAY CAME TO PASS, A REHEARSAL OF SORTS FOR a closing that by all evidence could not occur more than once per lifetime. For example: the last family supper, the last day of the summer season, the last sleepless night in your home, the last day before Leah disappeared across the Atlantic, the commitment of the Last Resort to memory.

By six o'clock, corporately speaking, the summer came to a close. The lifeguard stands were taken away, the food stands were boarded up with signs reading SEE YOU NEXT MEMORIAL DAY. The little planes that lugged signs behind them were wheeled into hangars, the Ferris wheel in Asbury Park stopped turning, the parking spaces along the avenue were suddenly vacant, newspapers blew in circles on the boardwalk, the awnings of the oceanfront houses were put in storage.

I walked along the deserted beach that evening before sunset. The water was still warm; September would be a pleasant month for drowning. I walked out to the end of Dennis's favorite jetty, in his company, and sat down to stare at the violet-colored horizon. Spain was out there somewhere.

The wind was cold, as was the ocean spray that crashed over the rocks of the jetty. Leah will be gone tomorrow, I thought, and sometime after that the Utopic deal will fall through. I looked up from the rocks to the horizon. Russia was also out there; they would be forced to retaliate. One afternoon missiles would appear, arching overhead; I would be walking with Dennis, holding hands with myself as the age encourages us each to do, and would see warheads reaming the firmament. "Technology," I told Dennis, "has succeeded in creating more ways for us to die together than our hearts and minds have created for us to live together."

Dennis's eyes implied that I was at best a singer/songwriter, not a thinker. I put my arm around his shoulder and said, "Cheer me up, kid! Do Leah for me!"

The little bastard stared at me—in the inimitable, curious way of the terrier—and promptly ran away.

THAT NIGHT THE ONLY LIGHT IN THE HOUSE CAME FROM THE kitchen. I walked through the darkness of the living room, cluttered as it was with piled furniture, and into illumination. The grandfather clock struck eight; Leah would be gone in fourteen hours.

Glenn Miller music was playing on the radio; Grandma was cooking on the stove, facing away. The kitchen table was covered with silver platters of food and the sink overflowed with dirty pots and pans.

Grandma turned. She wore a red apron over a formal black dress, red lipstick, pearl earrings and necklace. "I'm almost done, Whito!" she said musically. "You go call the others!"

I smiled bashfully. She'd done all this for Leah! "You didn't have to trouble yourself, Grandma."

"Where's Eunice, my colored girl? She's got to put the cake on Mommy's glass tray." She glanced around the room, baffled, and frowned. "Ain't Spud back from the Air Force yet? Well, you call Pop now. Call Pop to help Mom."

I studied her. "Grandma," I said softly, "it's Aldo. *Sonny.*"

She blinked at me, her wet eyes sparkling. I put my arms around her and led her gently to a chair.

"Ain't it sad." Her frightened eyes craved understanding. "Ain't everything just so sad it could kill a person like a gun."

She shook her head, pressing her lips together; then she laid her head as quietly as a child onto the table. It was clear to me that no one was coming. Grandma had cooked for the past, for the ghosts that had taken possession of her surrendering coherence.

I ASSISTED GRANDMA TO SADIE FISCHGRUND'S HOUSE NEXT door where she had stayed in a guest room ever since the house was sold to the Havermoores. When I returned to clean up the kitchen, Leah was picking at the salad with her fingers. "You really outdid yourself," she said.

We filled two plates and sat at the table, a single candle burning. "I want to tell you something," I said.

She nodded. I stared at her, wondering if it might possibly be the last time. She popped a beet into her mouth. "Best you've ever made."

"You'll miss my cooking, I bet."

She said she would. I kept still at unendurable length.

"I think you should hear what I learned this summer in your training school."

"O.K."

I stared, then scrutinized my fork. "I really learned a lot."

She told me she wouldn't mind hearing more.

"I learned that things in life—needs—are either necessary or unnecessary, sufficient or insufficient, or a combination of the two."

"Will I need a pencil and paper for this?"

"I learned that lots of things are sufficient but not necessary, and that very few things are necessary. I also learned that most things are unnecessary and insufficient. Further, I learned to identify the necessary things and what would make such things both necessary and sufficient, which is a neat trick."

"A student of Ms. Summit's summer school bears witness," Leah said proudly. I looked at her. "Continue," she said. "You are my favorite student."

"I learned that things are unnecessary if they interfere with what's necessary; for example, pride and selfishness." I stopped. She winked. I said, "Let me skip to the necessary but insufficient."

"Skip-ho."

"The necessary but insufficient things in my life, listed separately, are you, Dennis, my music succeeding, a place to lay me down to rest."

"Necessary but insufficient."

"With me so far?"

"Sex. What about sex?"

"That," I said, "would be listed, implicitly, under 'you' in the necessary column. Otherwise, sex is unnecessary, since it would interfere with my relationship with you, which is necessary."

"But can't two necessary things in life be incompatible?"

"Oh yes," I said. Leah waited for more. "Which means that life is an insoluble mess, a tragic little theater of selves, which is why you and I must stick together, why I should never worry about myself without worrying about you or vice versa." I closed one eye. "Have I learned?"

Leah didn't seem to make heads or tails of anything I'd said.

"In life," I resumed, "we at best struggle to maintain the necessary and most nearly sufficient. Life is putting up with what's never right."

Leah set to work on a piece of broccoli. "I guess my going

away throws a wrench in Mr. Keats' happiness machine?"

I nodded.

"Does that mean you won't forgive me once I go away?"

"One must forgiveth to geteth."

"You're just being tender because I'm going away and you're frightened."

"Also," I said, "because we only understand backwards. Once you mess up your life, it takes you a long time to understand what you did wrong."

Leah didn't say anything; I washed and she dried. After everything was put away, I said, "So? What do you say?"

Leah neatly folded the towel of her domestic participation and hung it on the rack above the sink. Then she looked at me. "Want to help me get my suitcase closed?"

VIII

GRANDMA WAS THE ONLY ONE ON THE BEACH THAT CLOUDY morning. The tide had reached a seasonal low and Grandma was seated well out in the strand's flat wet expanse. The wind was stiff and chilly; it rushed across the deserted beach and blew sand onto the avenue. The sea gulls, soaring in the gray sky, screamed as they dived for fish. Basically, I don't like endings of any kind. A sunset, for example, can be as frightening as a descending meat cleaver.

Grandma was dressed in a black bathing suit, skirted at the bottom, and a black bonnet dating from the age of kerosene lamps. She was composing a list. "Sonny," she said, "you love Grandma's candy sweets, don't you?"

I let her know how much.

She showed me a sheet of names. "I'm sending out my Thanksgiving invitations next week so nobody's got no excuses not to come to Grandma in Florida." She stared at me apprehensively. "Sonny ain't got plans for the holiday, does he?"

I said, "Yes, with Grandma in Florida."

She smiled. "Florida won't be so bad, sweetie. My Cuban

girl cleans good and don't steal from the house. Cubans is very honest people. They do the floors with a brush. Colored won't clean like that."

Well, I told Grandma that Leah had to get to the airport. She handed me an envelope labeled "Leah Summit." I peeked inside at the Spanish money when Grandma looked out to sea.

"It ain't so big to me as it used to be," she said. "It ain't so big as the sky. It ain't so big as the distance between Grandpa and me."

She opened her book, *From Here to Eternity*. She gazed at me somberly and turned to her place toward the end. "I'm almost finished, Sonny."

ELIOT HOWARD AND THE OLDER AND YOUNGER FIELDS WERE sweeping the floor of Leah's house. The new picture window was installed, the fireplace finished, the white walls newly painted. Beams of sunlight poured in from two sides of the house and crisscrossed in the living room. It really was an attractive little place, and there was every chance that Eliot and Teresa would be happy renting it. I hoped so.

Leah said good-bye to Eliot and the help, and I tried to heft the suitcase. Lumber Lee smiled sardonically when I resorted to both hands. Eliot gave her a small box wrapped in silver paper; so did Jack Fields. Leah stared at them and then at the boxes. Then she put her hand over her eyes.

I carried the suitcase and duffel bag to the car. I could do without the viewing of gifts.

When she got into the car, they waved, standing unhappily in line from the porch. The Airedale was tied to a porch post and began to whine. Leah said, "Oh God! I forgot," and ran back to kiss her, then kissed the three men again.

When she returned to the car, she was crying. I handed her

Grandma's envelope. She blew her nose into a red handkerchief and stuffed the envelope into her pocketbook, probably
thinking it a note from me.

We drove to the Beach House School so she could say
good-bye to Teresa. Afterward I asked, "Now your mother?"

"I said good-bye to her last night."

Well, I had said good-bye to her mother years ago.
"Grandma's on the beach," I said weakly. "Last stop."

I parked at the boarded-up snack stand. The clouds were
running gray and low. We could see Grandma at shoreline, the
only one on the beach.

Across the street, where the Last Resort once stood, a yellow
bulldozer had begun clearing ground for a new foundation.

Leah said "Right back" and scooted across the beach. I
watched her moving beneath the moving clouds, before the
moving sea. I bowed my head. The world is changing every
second: Maybe it takes us every second of our lives before we
get used to its mutable ways. Then, above the wind, above the
pounding waves and the damn bulldozer, I heard Leah's muted
voice crying, "Tramp! Tramp!"

I glanced up from the object of my concentration—a black
lever with the words EMERGENCY BRAKE inscribed on its surface—and saw the time flash on a digital watch on the dash-
board: 11:11.

IX

THE DAY AFTER GRANDMA'S FUNERAL, WITH MY ENTIRE FAMILY seated on the porch of our empty house, a man delivered a Mailogram to me. I read it once to myself, then folded it in half and asked Leah to come for a walk.

When the house was out of sight, I handed her the message.

DEAR TRAMP BOTTOMS:

I AM SORRY TO SAY THAT DUE TO A DISCONNECTED PHONE AT YOUR RESIDENCE I HAVE BEEN UNABLE TO CONTACT YOU DIRECTLY.

REGARDING YOUR DEMO, VERY TRAMP, UTOPIC RECORDS, THOUGH IT CANNOT OFFER YOU A RECORDING CONTRACT AT THIS TIME, WISHES TO PURCHASE THREE OF YOUR SONGS FOR RECORDING BY THREE OF ITS WELL-KNOWN ARTISTS.

PLEASE CONTACT ME AT ONCE AT 212-555-0488.

CONGRATS, J. DAYE

The sun was behind us, and our shadows, cast together on the sidewalk before us, seemed as vivid a symbol of our status as the world would ever bestow. When she turned to embrace me, I closed my eyes and imagined us projected as one even into that shadowy realm whither Grandma had gone. At the same time, I felt substantial for the first time in years.

Leah said gently, "I suppose it would be silly not to reexamine the details of our situation."

I said, "You know who you are and at last I've got a clue about myself," and assumed that by "details" Leah meant our quotidian battle with the world from now to ghosthood.

"Are you afraid?" Leah asked.

Her hand was in mine and my forehead rested upon her shoulder. Grandma whispered, Say no, Sonny; and so I did.

YOU REACH ADULTHOOD BY TRAVERSING A MINEFIELD. TRADI-tionally, those before you, those older than you, those closer to the end, lead the way by the tyrannies of custom and habit. What happens when those traditions crumble is something else again. If you are lucky, you make it anyway, and sometimes you are better off for it.

I was lucky. I had Leah Summit.

ABOUT THE AUTHOR

Born in 1951, SCOTT SOMMER was
raised in New Jersey and educated at
Ohio Wesleyan and Cornell universities.
His first novel, *Nearing's Grace,* was
published in 1979, and a collection of
short fiction, *Lifetime,* in 1981. Mr.
Sommer lives in New York City, where
he is currently writing two screenplays
and a book of novellas.